REBEL
WITH A
CUPCAKE

REBEL
WITH A
CUPCAKE

Anna Mainwaring

KCP Loft is an imprint of Kids Can Press

Kids Can Press gratefully acknowledges the financial support of the Government
of Ontario, through the Ontario Media Development Corporation.

Published in Canada and the U.S. by Kids Can Press Ltd.
25 Dockside Drive, Toronto, ON M5A 0B5

Kids Can Press is a Corus Entertainment Inc. company

www.kidscanpress.com
www.kcploft.com

The text is set in Minion Pro and Avenir Condensed Hand

Edited by Kate Egan
Designed by Emma Dolan
Jacket photo courtesy of Isabella Cassini / Alamy Stock Photo

Printed and bound in Altona, Manitoba, Canada in 1/2018 by Friesens Corp.

CM 18 0 9 8 7 6 5 4 3 2 1
CM PA 18 0 9 8 7 6 5 4 3 2 1

Library and Archives Canada Cataloguing in Publication

Mainwaring, Anna, author
Rebel with a cupcake / Anna Mainwaring.

ISBN 978-1-77138-826-9 (hardcover)
ISBN 978-1-5253-0033-2 (softcover)

I. Title.

PZ7.1.M35Reb 2018   j823'.92   C2017-903218-6

For Grace and Beth

CHAPTER ONE

Invisible Rule #1:
Sometimes being a girl sucks. And blows.
All at the same time.

"We've only got an hour," Hannah whimpers, grabbing the hair straighteners.

"Actually, it's 57 minutes and 39 seconds." Izzie peers at her phone. "38. 37. 36." Her bottom lip quivers and I think she's going to cry. "I don't think I can take the stress."

"I know," Hannah says. "Let's all phone in sick. Or pretend we've been abducted by aliens."

"Stop panicking," I suggest. "I mean, all we've got to do is get ready to go to school."

They both stare at me as if I've suddenly grown an extra head.

"Jess. Not now. Don't start the whole 'clothes are just clothes' thing. You may be right but surely even you can see that this is the worst day of the year." Hannah is now desperate, going through a pile of clothes on the sofa. We're in the basement of her house, where we always hang out, normally a happy place full of music, food and a very strong Wi-Fi connection.

Not so happy today.

Today is Own Clothes Day, the most nerve-racking day imaginable.

Izzie is in front of the mirror, putting on her fourth coat of mascara. She's going for the wicked-fairy-who's-fallen-on-hard-times look, and amazingly, she seems to pull it off. She looks like someone out of an advert — quirky yet glamorous all at the same time.

"You'd never guess you were a Manchester City fan until three months ago," I say.

Izzie humphs. She doesn't like to be reminded that she's made the bizarre transition from football fan to white witch. Not quite like Jadis in Narnia — we're short of polar bears and sleds round here — but she does think she can do magic. Worse still, most of our school believes her. But this means that she can go for the emo look and no one will hate her for it.

Next to her, with the dark red hair and pale complexion — that's Hannah. She's more conventionally dressed in a series of cunning layers that bring her in at the right places and out and up at the right places. With her big eyes and ringlets, she looks a bit like a Disney princess. But whereas Disney princesses are never famous for having much going on between their ears, Hannah is on course for eleven A-pluses in her national exams. Clearly not just a pretty face …

Hannah turns around and stares at her backside.

"Do my slag lines show?" she asks.

I look closely, as only a best friend can at another friend's arse, to see if her panties are visible. "Nope," I say, "you pass the slag test."

She smiles contentedly and goes back to work on her eyebrows. I'm saying nothing, but in a few minutes, it'll look like two slugs are sitting on top of her eyes. For an intelligent girl, she clearly doesn't mind drawing on fake eyebrows that make her look — well, to be honest — a bit stupid.

Then there's me. Jesobel — Jess for short. I sort of like my name cos it sounds pretty. But older people always look shocked when they're introduced to me. Apparently, the original Jezebel was some woman from the Bible who got executed for doing magic, and then her dead body was fed to the dogs. Not really a lifestyle to aspire to.

But maybe it's my name that's marked me out as a bit different. Because while these two are in crisis, I'm just sitting here reading the latest post on my favorite blog, *Fat Girl with Attitude*.

That is until Izzie says, "And what are you wearing today?"

I look at her, bemused. "Er, this?" I wave a hand in the general direction of my body.

"You're Year Eleven! That's what Year Nine will be wearing!" Hannah cries.

I look down at my so-called skinny jeans and Hollister top. She has a point — I have been wearing the same outfit for the last two years. (Don't worry, it has been washed. I don't mean LITERALLY wearing it for two years — that would be gross.)

Izzie grabs my bag. "Let's see what else you've got. Did you bring the leggings?" She rummages through it, tossing one garment aside and then grabbing the next with glee. "Yes!" she cries, and I'm sent to the corner to change clothes. Apparently, layered T-shirts, short skirt and leggings are so much better than what I had on before. With a sigh, I add my prefect badge to my new and improved outfit. I get to stalk the corridors at lunchtime and report any bad behavior.

"That is so much better," Hannah reports back. I stare at myself in the mirror. A girl rather larger than Hannah stares back. But she's smiling, so that's okay. Some might say she's fat, and on a bad day, I'd agree with them. I'm not a whale, mind, just, you know, curvy. And curves are good, aren't they? I've read many blog posts telling me that, but then the photos of curvy women that go alongside them show women that have clearly never eaten ice cream or even thought about a chip. My idea of curves is having boobs that actually wobble when you run upstairs.

I digress. You might be wondering why there's so much fuss over what we're wearing, and you know, I'm kind of with you on this one. But then again … let's think it over for a minute.

Take an all-girls' school and stick it in a reasonably posh area — South Manchester — stuffed full of football players (and their perma-tanned wives), doctors, dentists, lawyers, TV presenters and artists, who all want their darling daughters to be the BEST. It's like *The Hunger Games* without the bows and arrows — a fight to the death to be the cleverest, thinnest, prettiest, most popular girl in the school.

So, it's bad enough on a normal day when we have to wear regulation uniform — gray skirt, gray blazer, gray socks. (I think they want our souls to be gray.) Own Clothes Day is worse, much worse. Every detail of what we wear will be noted, analyzed and posted online within seconds of us arriving at school, accompanied by mean comments if we've got it wrong. This is why Hannah and Izzie are freaking out. But even though I know all of this, I'm still not that bothered. I mean, there are more important things in the world than clothes, aren't there?

And by things I mean food. Now that I'm dressed, I'm feeling a bit hungry and thinking that food might lighten the mood.

"I know what will make things just tickety-boo," I say. (I know it's an old-fashioned word. I was brought up mostly by my grandmother. This shows from time to time.) I pick up the plastic container that I have carefully carried from my house, a few streets away, and tease open the lid.

Izzie and Hannah simultaneously sigh as if they have both just seen the most beautiful sight in the world. Which they have, if I do say so myself.

I know what you're thinking — we're girls and food is bad because food makes us fat. That's the invisible rule, isn't it? If you're a teenage girl, you should hate your body, hate food and hate yourself.

Well, I don't think like that.

I don't get why food is the enemy. Have you noticed that people are often nicer when they're sitting around eating and talking, rather than not eating and being miserable? Yes, Cat, if you ever get around to reading this, I do mean you.

And also food never lets me down. And there aren't too many things you can say that about.

Cupcakes eaten and clothes sorted, it's on to hair and makeup. Within seconds, the basement is full of the familiar smells of teenage girls: scorched hair, body spray and scented lip gloss.

Finally, Hannah stops looking terrified. "Okay, we're fine for time and we all look great. Result."

We stare at our reflections in the mottled mirror that hangs on the wall of the basement. Three cool but different girls smile back.

"Come on, time to go," Izzie says, and that's that. Let the games begin ...

CHAPTER TWO

Invisible Rule #2:
If a girl has curly hair, she wants straight. If she's short,
she wants to be tall. If she's got no boobs, she wants huge ones.
You're never allowed to be happy with what you've got.

We head down the high street as slowly as possible. No one wants to look too keen, and the walk to school is the best opportunity, today of all days, to see who's wearing what and whether anyone is really way out there. Like the year Sonia Fitzherbert came wearing her mum's wedding dress and full white body makeup. Apparently, she was being some weirdo — from a book by Dickens — who never got over not getting married. Online dating didn't exist back in the dark ages.

As a team, Hannah, Izzie and I attempt to check out Ruth Mulholland and Sara Ejaz, also from our year, who walk parallel to us on the other side of the road. They look at us, we look at them. We're wearing the same kind of stuff. But not exactly the same. That would be the Worst Thing That Could Happen.

We wave at each other and give the thumbs-up. We try to be nice, whereas we know that some other girls will just do THE LOOK. You know, where they scan you up and down with a pinched face like they've got a mouthful of sour candy, and you know they're doing a checklist of your faults.

Recipe for the Perfect Girl (according to fashion shoots and celebrity sites):

1. Legs: thigh gap required. Also, absolutely NO suggestion that hair ever grows on these babies at all. Ever.

2. Boobs: need to look like small firm jellies that point up; absolutely NO hint of nipples.

3. Skin: airbrushed perfection.

4. Hair: must look natural in a way that only three hours in front of a mirror and twenty products can create.

5. Stomach: flat and hard enough to roll pastry on.

I could go on — but I can't bear to. Far more interesting are two boys from the boys' school who are our FRIENDS but not our BOYFRIENDS. We are invited over by those most romantic words, "Hey, wenches."

Dominic Hall and Fred Cormack are lounging on a bench. We've known each other for years. In fact, I married Dom in the playhouse one lunchtime back in Year Two, so I'll assume that the "wench" comment is ironic. We do fool around at parties if there's no one else we fancy. I like him, but he doesn't make my heart race.

"Looking good, girls," Dom says as he checks us out, up and down, apparently appreciating all our efforts.

"Of course," Hannah says with a well-practiced flick of her hair, "we always look good."

Which is weird. Even with our friends-who-happen-to-be-boys, Hannah has suddenly changed from a normal person into a smirking robot.

"So, did you hear about …" Fred leans in with the latest news. Boys may say they don't gossip, but they're just as bad as us.

While I'm half listening to what Girl B might have done or not done to Boy A, I can't help thinking about all the time we three have put into our appearance this morning (the clothes, the hair, the makeup), when Dom and Fred have clearly just squirted on the Lynx and they're good to go. I don't think Fred has even brushed his hair — this year — and Dom has spots. A girl would struggle to leave the house without twenty layers of concealer on them, but Dom clearly still loves himself. If reincarnation does exist, I want to come back as a boy. At least then, when I fart in public, everyone will find it funny.

Then I notice how Dom stares at my boobs. There are a variety of ways to look at this:

a) I'm getting male attention. In public, for all to see. Which is good and makes me look good in the eyes of all the girls walking past, who WILL be taking notice.

Or

b) How rude — there is more to me than my mammary glands. But given that I am, you know, on the large side, some girls would think that I'm lucky to get any guy to notice me. Weirdly, it's girls who give me grief for being fat, not boys.

"You can look at my face, you know," I say to him.

He laughs and hits me on the arm.

"Sorry," he says, "but I'm a boy. I'm just a testosterone machine, hardwired to look at breasts. And yours are just amazing. Are you sure that you've not had a boob job this year?"

I sigh and then I blush more than just a bit, not sure how to take this. I mean, this is good, isn't it? But do I want to be liked just for some random genetic factor that means I've not seen my feet for the last year?

"How many times do I have to tell you? I haven't had a boob job — all my hormones just kicked in at once!"

"Well, my hormones like what your hormones are doing to your body," he says cheerfully, punching me on the arm again to show that this is just joking and not flirting. I think. Or am I missing something? I could just do with my arm being punched less.

As he turns back to the others, I carefully glance around to see if a certain boy is there. A boy who makes my heart, face and other parts of my anatomy tingle if I see him. You see, I have a bit of a secret crush on this guy called Matt Paige. Who, unfortunately, is not in sight.

I do mean secret. I would actually rather die than tell anyone. And I do mean crush because the amount of time I think about him puts me into the category of Scary Stalker Girl.

And this is how it happened. How I fell ridiculously head over heels for him. It only took a second.

He lives near me. About a year ago, he was walking home and I was in my room, doing my homework in a distracted sort of way — well, I was just looking out of the window. And I looked down at him. He looked up at me.

And he smiled.

At me.

That was it. That was all it took.

All of a sudden, I realized that under that mad mop of hair, he was hot. With a good smile. And I sort of glowed inside. It was one of the first times ever that a boy actually looked at me and smiled. As if I was pretty. It was lovely!

Of course, reality kicked in later and I realized that I'd been sitting down and so all he saw was my face. And if you just see my face, I don't look fat. If you just see my face, I look a bit like my mum. But I can't just be a face. The rest of me is attached. I can't push myself to school sitting on a wheelie chair with a desk in front of me to disguise the rest.

But for months now, he's been all I can think about. He's in Year Twelve at the boys' school, so he's an older man! You can tell a lot from a boy's A-level choices, and his are: Psychology (in touch with his feelings), English Literature (you have to be a real man to do English at the boys' school — imagine the piss-taking), French (swoon) and, wait for it — Art (double swoon). What a combination — perfect or what? He's interested in human nature, he's creative, bilingual and actually confesses to reading books! I know all this because Hannah's elder brother, Alex, is in his year and she found all this out for me. It took me ages to ask all the right questions so that she told me everything without realizing that I fancied him.

Even though I'm fine about … well, the way I look; I'm also a realist. I'm me and he's him and there's very little chance of anything happening. There might be if I looked a bit more like that girl over there — a vision of female perfection, lounging on a low wall, surrounded by tall, cute boys. All our group are suddenly staring at her.

She's the girl that everyone wants to be or be with. She's thin, she's pretty and she has those huge eyes that look too big for her face. She's wearing shiny leggings and manages that winning combination of sexy and vulnerable. The boys competing for her attention are perfect. Tall, hot, old, but not too old. And guess what? They look her in the eye. Because somehow, being attractive means that boys make more effort with you. You're worth it.

Her tinkling laugh chimes out and, for a split second, her dark eyes break away from the group and scan lightly over us. I have a strange feeling when I watch her. Since I was little, I've watched all the films, happy in the knowledge that all I have to do is to be myself and I will be loved. Except, in films, "being yourself" also means being impossibly thin with ridiculously large eyes and perfect hair.

A bit like that girl on the wall.

Dom sighs deeply. He looks back at me and shakes his head, polite enough for once not to say what I've heard so many times: *How can you two be sisters?*

"Yeah, yeah, yeah," I say. "But Cat's out of your league."

"Not in my head, she's not." He grins wickedly and winks, and I'm not sure whether to be shocked or to laugh. I laugh — it's generally the best way to handle anything.

According to the big clock over the row of shops, we have seven minutes to get to school. If we move up a gear from dawdle to walk, we'll get there in time. The boys drift off, casting longing looks at Cat. She doesn't look at me again. She pretty much ignores me all the time. This has been going on for about a year, since around the time she stopped eating. Which was about the time she left St. Ethelreda's and started doing the A-level exams that will get her to university. She's in sixth form college. With boys. St. Ethelreda's is only for girls, because apparently, we can't be trusted around the opposite sex.

Hannah catches my eye and I shrug. We've talked about Cat so many times that there's nothing more to say. But as we stroll up the hill to school, I do fantasize about force-feeding her a whole plate of my very best cupcakes until she balloons to — OMG — my size. Would boys still look past me to her the way they do now?

As I'm about to enter the school gates, Hannah puts a warning hand on my arm. It's Mrs. Brown, Assistant Head with Special Responsibility for Child Intimidation, standing by the main entrance. She can normally be found striding down corridors like the Snow Queen, sucking the life-spirit out of all who cross her path. I swear even teachers hide behind corners to get away from her.

I'm not usually so horrible, but she is the nastiest person who ever lived. It's not just that she's mean, but that she seems to enjoy being mean. The more the Year Sevens cry when she screams at them for forgetting to button up their blazers (I know, what a terrible crime — an undone button!), the more she smiles. And there are no rules against a teacher who's a bully.

So, there she is, standing guard at the gate, nostrils flared, looking out for anything that's visible that shouldn't be. Cos that's one of the many things that drives her crazy — female flesh on show. Just behind her, her latest victims stand cowed. Their crimes are easy to guess. Quivering Amy Dutton? Too much cleavage. Sniveling Julie Macdonald? Midriff visible. Defiant Catherine Temple? Skirt like a belt. Likely punishment for dressing like this? Well, at the end of the school year, we have a Leavers' Ball. It's the highlight of the year where we all celebrate the fact that we can finally leave this fascist institution and go to sixth form college (a practice version of university but you don't actually leave home), where we will be treated like adults for the first time in our lives. But these girls — they can kiss going to Leavers' goodbye. And that means their social lives have just died.

Just as we get close, one of the younger teachers walks past. Mrs. Brown's eyes scan her like a laser, taking in the pencil skirt, the high heels and the fitted cardigan. Her eyes narrow. "Miss Farrow. See me after attendance," Brown bellows.

Poor Miss Farrow bites her ruby lips and looks petrified. We sigh for her. She'll learn. Even female teachers have to avoid any suggestion that they might be attractive. Not that I really want to go there — I mean, they're teachers, after all. As we rush past Mrs. Brown, we hear an intake of breath as she looks at Izzie, but we're saved. A scream and a whimper break out behind us.

"Charlotte Harrison, are those FISHNET tights? FISHNETS? Get yourself over here."

And another is sacrificed so we can go free.

Izzie sighs. "She'd prefer it if we all wore nuns' habits and then nothing would be on show."

So, it's 8:49 a.m. and we seem to have survived so far.

But I speak too soon because as we climb up the stairs to our form room, Izzie spots danger ahead. "Oh no," she says, "here they come."

And the next trial begins.

So, we've just got past the psychopath teacher. Now meet the students who are most like her. Just a bit prettier.

Meet Zara, Tara, Lara, Tilly and Tiff.

I could try to describe their individual characteristics, but they all get confused in my head. Just imagine a many-headed Hydra from a horror film, each snake's head with perfect makeup and straightened hair. Once upon a time, I was quite friendly with Lara. But this was before she discovered Tara and Zara, and their personalities merged, and all Lara's nice bits got lost in the mix.

Let me sum them up:

1. They stalk through the corridors as if on a catwalk, trailing perfume, money and attitude as they pout and pose, making lesser girls leap out of their way.

2. They talk loudly so everyone has to overhear the precise details of their interactions with boys, all designed to make you feel inferior if your last close encounter with a potential romantic partner was buying a skinny hot chocolate from a Starbucks barista.

3. They tease you if you haven't had sex. #virgin

4. They tease you if you have had sex. #slut

5. They don't like anyone. I don't think they even like themselves.

They file past us on the stairs, sniggering.

"Nice look, Izzie," Tara simpers. "You'll need a love potion to get anyone to fancy you in that getup."

Hannah they merely ignore.

Zara checks me up and down with a deliberate stare. "My oh my, we all know you like your sweets, Jess, but it's really starting to show."

"Wow," I say, and as they walk on, giggling, I shout, "Oh, by the way, you should ask Tilly what she was doing with Jamie in the park last night." (You have to use whatever ammunition comes your way.)

Zara spins around, her eyes like a snake, while poor Tilly begins to tremble.

Then Zara runs lightly down a few steps and stands, staring, over me. "You fat cow," she says, sneering. I laugh in her face and turn away from her. Then I'm not quite sure what happens. Does she push me? Does someone push her into me? All I know is that I'm flying backward and I land hard on my backside.

"At least you have a soft landing," Zara purrs. As she turns, she flicks a glance back over me. "As I said, it's starting to show."

I look down and see that my leggings have ripped at the seam, from halfway down my thigh to my calf, revealing a huge expanse of white flesh. Zara stares at me in triumph and waltzes off. At least waxing my legs last night was a good idea.

Even so: Bullies–1, Jess–0.

CHAPTER THREE

Invisible Rule #3:
If a pupil doesn't do their work, they get detention.
If a teacher doesn't mark work, nothing happens.
There is no such thing as teacher detention.

Hannah sits down next to me on the stairs as I rub my sore backside.

"Are you all right?" she asks. "Shall we tell Mrs. Carroway?"

I give her a look. "I'm not going to a form tutor about anything. We are not Year Sevens. I'll get my own back on her somehow, don't you worry." With that, I hoist myself back up, my ego hurting more than my bum. And THAT is killing me.

Other girls filter past, some with soft whispers, others calling out, "Okay, Jess?"

Sporty Amy T. jogs by. "Don't worry, Jess. I've got General PE with Zara this afternoon. I'll take her down then! She can run but she can't hide." She trots on with a wink.

The three of us look down at my ripped leggings. The intake of breath from Hannah and Izzie confirms that it's worse than I thought.

"Shall we try the Textiles room?" Izzie says hopefully, but I can see straight away that the material is too frayed to sew back together properly. There is just a sea of bare white leg. I didn't think the leggings were that tight.

Then a thought hits me like a thunderbolt. A calorie-laden, carb-enriched, fat-loaded thunderbolt. What if Zara is right? What if I've just gone from "Well, I can just about live with that" to "We don't stock your size here. Why don't you try the FAT shop next door for FAT people"?

While I'm thinking the unthinkable, my friends are attempting to sort out my problem. "Let's ask around. Someone's bound to have something spare to wear, and leggings, well, they fit anyone," Izzie says helpfully.

I look at the legs filing past and notice, not for the first time of course, that they're all a lot thinner than mine. The difference is that this time I care.

The school bell rings and now we're officially late for attendance, but that's okay because Mrs. Carroway is *always* late. So I go to the toilets and take off the leggings. I wish I'd worn my jeans. As I look in the mirror, I feel horribly exposed. This skirt is too short to wear without tights or leggings. I can live with my legs when they're covered up. But au naturel? I think not.

The door of the loo bangs open, and who should come in but Catamaran Caroline (so-called because she was once overheard saying, "Daddy's thinking of buying a catamaran this weekend" in the same way your or my dad might think of buying a Meatloaf album. In case you don't know, a catamaran is some kind of weird boat that not even idiots can capsize. They cost A LOT). She gives me the once-over, then makes a face like she's seen some sick. How many more people are going to look at me like that today?

As a result of all this, I am three minutes late for attendance.

And guess what? Just this once, Mrs. Carroway's on time. She usually swans in ten minutes late with a Starbucks in her hand, but today, she's already sitting at the computer, logged on and ready to go. She attempts to give me (queen of the stare) a hard stare.

It fails.

She starts calling out the messages for the day and doesn't seem to notice the amount of leg that I'm showing. So, I just sit down.

That's when she calls on me. "Jesobel, it's not like you to be late. I'll let this one go but you'll be getting a letter home if it happens again."

Oh God, I'm quaking in my Vans. A letter. In the twenty-first century, the school attempts to communicate our sins to parents via paper letters. They don't seem to notice that no one ever replies to these letters. Because parents never actually get them. Cos we steal them. There you go: School–0, Students–1.

My other friends try to offer help. There's Sana — small, huge eyes, constantly readjusting her headscarf and trying to copy homework. She's always drawing manga when she should be studying. Then Suzie — funny, long legs, never hands her homework in on time. Never listens to her parents from what I can see. Finally, Bex. She finds school hard. She finds life hard. Give her a hockey stick and she's transformed. But even she feels sorry for me today.

The bell rings. So, with naked legs, it's off to English. I hope it's not one of those lessons where you're made to put Post-its on the board.

There are generally two kinds of teachers — young ones who've been on courses and try to make you do stuff in an "interesting" way, and old ones who just get on with it with as little fuss as possible, unless the inspectors are in. Fortunately, Mrs. Lewis is one of the old ones. She just puts some questions on the board and leaves us to work through them, so my legs can stay safely hidden behind my desk.

Unfortunately, this gives her time to check who's done their homework.

"Jesobel, I'm still missing an essay from you from last week."

What I really want to say is, *I'll hand it in when you mark my controlled assessment, which you've had for four weeks.* I mean, *I'm* in trouble for not doing *my* work, but I'm not allowed to say to her, "That's not good enough, Mrs. Lewis. You're in detention."

I just don't buy that line teachers give us about being so busy. I whisper to Izzie, "Funny how when we walk past her house, she's always drinking white wine and watching *Come Dine with Me.* Busy, my aching arse!"

I might have whispered this too loudly, because now Mrs. Lewis is looking at me as if I've just said Shakespeare is overrated.

"What did you just say, Jesobel?" she snaps.

"I was just saying how moving I found this poem," I lie. Then I put on the wounded puppy expression. "Sorry about the homework, miss. I'll hand it in tomorrow."

"I expect better from one of my prefects," she says sharply.

And I feel like screaming, cos today's been quite trying and it's not even nine o'clock yet. But I smile sweetly while I imagine her drowning in a vat of crisp white wine, her little arms waving as she bobs pathetically, sinking deeper and deeper into the alcohol. Just cos I'm a prefect — a dubious honor at the best of times — I'm supposed to be bloody perfect.

"Well," she says with a cold smile, "if I can't mark your work, I can't tell if you're on target for your predicted grade. So, you'd better go and sit with the girls who are below target."

The whole class draws in a deep breath.

Thing is, in our school you sit in order.

Those who are pretty perfect — you can tell by their neat handwriting and beautifully selected stationery items — and are going to get A's or A-pluses are in one group. I'm always in this group, partly because I work hard and partly because I really do love those cute Japanese erasers shaped like kittens. Then there are the more normal girls who are going to get B's and, hell, maybe a few C's. And there's the rest —

D's or below. The lost causes. The girls who just don't get it. They look sad, like rescue puppies that no one wants. This system is supposed to encourage us to stay out of the bottom group.

I can feel words bubbling up inside me like lava in a volcano. But I don't say a word. I just move myself, my books, my bag, my pencil case with all its lovely color-coded pens, and sit down at the Fail Table. With Ellie Unwin, who smells, and not in a nice way. And Rosie Sherwood, who cries all the time. Shall we review the situation?

1. I'm wearing a skirt that makes me feel ridiculous. #fashionfail

2. Most days I don't feel fat. Today I do.

3. The hypocrisy and double standards today have gone from "mildly annoying" to "this place is driving me crazy."

4. Normal Me would just go, "Hey, having a bad day? Then eat an amazing cake!" Current Me doesn't want cake.

This situation is going from bad to worse.

CHAPTER
FOUR

Observation #1:
Doing what you're told is often overrated.

I put my head down and answer a series of devious questions about a poem that seems to me to be a random swirl of words on a page but apparently is a work of genius cos some dead white guy wrote it.

It makes me feel slightly better that Ellie and Rosie, my fellow public failures, really can't do this. I know the BS that the exam board wants and can puke up pages of it, but Ellie is chewing her pen in a sad sort of way and adding smiley faces to all the *i*'s in her work, while Rosie is weeping into her homework planner. I push my book so that Rosie can see it and nod to her to copy. She almost smiles but not quite.

Meanwhile, at the non-failing tables, Sana chats away to Bex for pretty much all of the lesson and so keeps Mrs. Lewis's attention away from us and our cheating. Note to any teachers out there — don't worry about the noisy ones, they're easy to spot. It's the quiet ones you need to watch.

The bell screeches at the end of the lesson, drowned out by the sound of exercise books and pencil cases being flung into bags. Izzie comes and stands next to me, making a sad face.

"I'll curse her if you like," she offers.

"You'd do that for me?" I laugh. "You're so sweet. Can I order boils or being hit by lightning?"

"You laugh at me," Izzie says, "but you know what I can do."

(Once she did a talk in English about a "love potion" and gave it to Rebecca Turner. Who then snogged Jay Hudsworth at a party. Yes, Rebecca Turner — not cool — snogged Jay Hudsworth — way cool. Izzie puts it down to her love potion. I put it down to vodka. The rest of the school is undecided.)

We wander off into the main corridor, knocked about like corks in the sea as we are hit by a series of large bags carried by Year Sevens. The size of their bags increases in direct proportion to their smallness. I'm sure you could turn this into a mathematical equation — which would then be the only useful thing done in a Maths lesson this century.

Izzie stops to talk to someone while I plow on up the stairs to Music. I'm not really in the mood for chitchat. My legs feel naked and huge. I'm in the mood for an argument.

As I stand at the top of the steps, I see my reflection in an ancient glass cabinet. I see my legs in all their glory. Yuck. I really am half dressed. In fact, I have unwittingly achieved the slut look that half of Year Eleven aims for on a Friday night. I look like I should be in some music video, bumping, grinding and generally getting my groove on behind some hip-hop star.

"Wicked look," Sana calls, and gives me a wolf whistle. I do a little shimmy in return. I might not feel great about myself at this precise moment, but I can still pretend that I think I'm awesome. I'm not beaten yet. I mean, what's the big deal about a pair of big, naked legs?

"Work it, girlfriend," she continues and, giggling, I pretend that I'm on an imaginary catwalk, sashaying and spinning, blowing kisses to the invisible paparazzi. There's quite a few of us on the stairs and in the corridor, and the chant of "Go, Jess" begins to build as I continue to shake my thing.

Sana laughs as I spin and pout at her. She gets her phone out and starts to film me. "You got it, Jess!"

For the first time all day, I actually feel okay.

It's then I hear a cold laugh.

"Exactly what do you think you are doing, Jess Jones?"

I look down and see *her* again. Zara. Her hair groomed to perfection, labels dripping off her extra-small clothing. Everything I despise. Smirking as she looks up at me.

"How can you bear to look at yourself in the mirror?" she spits out. "You are just so fat now — you're grotesque."

My heart starts to pound. Everyone is watching now. Before, it was just a spat, but now I feel like everyone's waiting for me to say something good. Too bad my brain has stopped working, along with my mouth. Because the things she is saying are the things that I never say to myself. Except today.

I've had enough.

Adrenaline rushes through me and I'm spoiling for a fight. My backside still hurts and I've had a rubbish morning. All cos of her.

Even prefects bite back sometimes.

I march down the steps until I face her. I can sense a few others just behind me.

"Grotesque, Zara?" I hiss. "That's a big word for you — do you think you can spell it?"

She starts to speak but I stop her.

"I might be fat but I can change that if I want. But you, you will always be a bitch."

She starts forward — is she going for me again? God, this girl has anger issues.

But I'm not falling for it this time. So, I just step back.

Which means that Zara — arm outstretched to slap me, pull my hair or inflict some other girly form of physical abuse — flies through the air and lands on the floor at my feet.

"Hurrah," I say in mock triumph. "Fat Girls–1, Bullies–0." And I put my foot on her arse before she has time to move, pumping my arms like I've just won a boxing match. Which I suppose I have. Around me, there are a few cheers and whoops. Zara pushes my foot away and leaps up, her face twisted in fury, mascara starting to run down her face in dirty rivers.

I almost feel sorry for her. But she did push me earlier and she would have done it again. I just got out of the way.

"I'll get you for this." With that, she shoves her way through the crowd, Tilly and Tiff trailing behind her.

I look up at the small crowd on the stairs.

"Okay — show's over, people."

Most girls are laughing, smiling, giving me the thumbs-up.

"Nice one, Jess. You showed her, for once," Sana says.

I can't help noticing Hannah hasn't said a word.

"She deserved it," I say defensively.

"I know," Hannah says, "but it just didn't feel like you just then."

I grimace. I know what she means. I'm not one of the mean girls normally. It almost felt like I was being Zara and she was being me.

This thought occupies me during most of Music and then break.

And then, later, when everyone around me is telling me I did well, but I'm not so sure, that's when I hear the shout of doom.

"Jesobel Jones. Get. Yourself. Here. Now."

It's Mrs. Brown, Assistant Head from Hell. She's standing a few feet away from me in the hall and pointing to the place just in front of her feet. Without even meaning to, I wander over.

At first, I'm not sure what she's going on about. As I stand in front of Mrs. Brown, it's like standing in a wind tunnel. She screams, she yells, she goes red. Spit flies in my face.

"You. Are. A. Nasty. Piece. Of. Work," she shouts. Apparently, she can only communicate in one-word sentences when angry.

I turn to Hannah, who looks back at me in shock.

"You. Are. A. Bully," she continues.

Okay, I think I need to introduce her to a concept called irony. I mean, she's calling *me* a bully?

"I've got Zara Lovechild sobbing in my office, bruises covering her arms. You did this to her."

I try to say something.

"Don't deny it. I saw it on the school cameras."

Zara might have been sobbing in her office a few moments ago, but now she's standing just behind Mrs. Brown and smiling at me in triumph through her messed-up makeup.

"Did you, or did you not, call her a bitch?"

"Yes, but —"

"I have no time for buts. You verbally and physically assaulted a fellow pupil. Get to my office now. And while we are there, we'll discuss what you're wearing. Because to put it simply: You. Are. Too. Fat. To. Wear. That. Skirt. You look ridiculous."

Two bullies are accusing me of bullying, when I was just standing up for myself. And now a fat woman is calling me fat.

End of.

That's when I have my moment of madness.

I turn and walk away.

Then there's more screaming.

"Don't. You. Walk. Away. From. Me. Jesobel. Jones."

I keep walking.

"One more step and you'll be suspended. You've got your national exams in a few weeks."

I take three more for good measure. I might as well be committing suicide but she's just pushed me over the edge. As I dash up the stairs,

I sense bodies behind me. The students of the school are somehow managing to slow her down. Even with a head start, I don't fancy my chances. This is more exercise than I'm used to. Out of breath, I turn a corner and see a cleaners' cupboard. Hiding suddenly seems a good idea so I open the door and dive inside. A little Year Seven, coming down the corridor toward me with the most enormous bag I've ever seen, looks at me in surprise. I put my finger to my lips as I close the door.

Inside my cupboard, I hear the drumming of feet — Brown is in full chase mode. I'm almost sad that I'm hiding in a cupboard, as I would have liked to see her run. "Did you see her? Did Jesobel Jones come this way?" the voice of Brown booms.

A trembly voice replies, "A girl ran that way, miss."

"Get. That. Ridiculous. Bag. Out. Of. My. Way. Now."

The footsteps fade away.

I peer out and smile at the little girl, who grins back as she waves her bag in triumph. School–1, Brown–0.

But then my smile fades quickly. I've run away from Brown. What do I do next? Opposite me is a huge cabinet full of trophies that celebrate everything girls have ever done in this school that's worth celebrating. But all I can see is my reflection in the glass. This morning, I looked in the mirror with my friends and I smiled back. Now, I see myself full length, and let's just say, I'm not smiling anymore. Is this how people see me every day? I wish I were invisible.

But I am Jess Jones and I will not be beaten. Enough of feeling sad. I brush away my stupid tears and plan how to make this day better. It's time for a prison break. I want to go home. It's that simple.

Once I've made my mind up, the rest is easy. I quickly find the back stairs, then run down the fire escape and out into the grounds. Frantic waving at the window grabs my attention. Sana and Hannah mouth at me, "What are you doing?" and "Come back." Not a chance. I've had enough of being looked at. Sana furiously motions to me to come back in. I shake my head and then she points at me and pretends to cut her throat. She clearly thinks I'm crazy to do this. But this feels so good when I was feeling so bad before.

So, I ignore my law-abiding friends and I push the recycling bins next to the wall and I climb up. The drop down to the road looks a bit scary, but not as scary as going back inside. If I don't make a move, they'll find me.

I kneel on the wall, then sit on my bum and let my legs swing down. I take a big breath. I drop down and then I'm standing on the pavement. On the wrong side of the wall. With no way back.

In the street, it's calm and quiet. My heart is pounding.

I look at my watch. 11:33 a.m. My phone is going crazy in my pocket, but I have a very unusual craving for home so I turn it off. Dad won't be up yet; Mum will be at the gym. If I walk quickly, I might just have time to get home to watch some black-and-white film with Gran before she has her first whiskey.

And, today, I think I might just join her.

CHAPTER
FIVE

Observation #2:
Ever noticed how childish adults can be?

In the quiet street outside the school walls, there are no cars, a few trees and more dog poo than is necessary in any so-called civilized country. An old lady walks past and smiles at me. It is all very normal. Apart from me.

I wonder how I appear to the old lady. Do I look like a fugitive from justice? Or a criminal, or worse, a bully? Or do I just look like what I am — a red-faced teenage girl who's missing a pair of leggings?

My heart is still hammering away. I remember learning something about cardiac arrests in Biology and I wonder if that's what's happening to me. I feel like I'm in one of those futuristic films where anything could happen. For a moment, I lean against a tree and concentrate on my breath coming in and out. We did some lesson on relaxation once, but the teacher just lost it cos Abbie Norman kept farting.

No one from school has come to find me yet. So, I have four choices, right?

1. I can go back to school and face the consequences now.

2. I can go home and face the consequences later.

3. I can go into town, draw out my entire finances (£245.31), get on a train and see how far that gets me. (I don't have a passport on me, so that limits my options.)

4. I can drop out of school and hang around some bus stops for the next year or two. Maybe have a kid or two and live on benefits. (If the *Daily Mail* can be believed.)

After a bit of thought, I decide that number 2 suits me best at the moment. Number 1 is probably the most sensible, but being sensible is clearly not a course that I'm following today. I'm going for crash and burn. I left home a prefect, a student considered sensible and capable. At some point during the morning, I became a bully. And then I talked back to the teacher and left without permission. In other schools, this might be quite common. At our school, not so much. At our school, it's considered outrageous not to open a door for a teacher and throw yourself down face-first so they can walk over your back.

Part of me expects to see Brown staked out in front of the house with a black hood on her head, a noose in her hand and a smile on her face, ready to hang me from the nearest streetlamp.

The more rational part of me knows that the phone call from school to home has already happened and it's just a matter of time before it catches up with me.

As I turn down my street, there's an empty space outside our house where Mum's car is normally parked, so she's at the gym (even though she's been running already) or "networking" with the SOWs (Skinny Old Women). Networking seems to involve the drinking of industrial amounts of prosecco, but it's a bit early for that. Dad's car's there but I suspect that he's not up yet. He was the guitar player in a band that was a three-hit wonder in the nineties. He's not like a regular dad.

But there's no strange car outside the house. No one has tracked me back to my lair yet. As I open the front door, I hear Lauren's voice. My little sister's on the telephone. Still in her grubby pajamas, she has jammy toast in one hand (and mostly smeared over her face) and her soother, snuggly and the house phone in the other. She is deep in conversation with whoever's at the other end.

"Gran smells of wee," she says with great confidence to the person unknown on the telephone. "And she's a poo-poo head." I can hear the person on the other end of the phone speaking slowly, but Lauren just keeps talking. "And she's lazy cos she never gets out of her chair. I don't like Gran cos she's mean to Alice and I don't like anyone who's mean to Alice." As she says this, her face crumples and tears begin to form in the corners of her eyes. It's like she's read a book on How to Make Grown-Ups Feel Sorry for You and Therefore Do Everything You Want.

Lauren's eyes well up, her mouth turns into an O and her shoulders start to shake. "She said Alice was silly and she had to stand outside. But it's cold outside and I can hear Alice crying. And it makes me SAAADDD …" This final word turns into a wail and she drops the phone in her misery. A disembodied voice starts to ask questions. I hang up ASAP and I hug Lauren while enormous sobs rack her little body. She snuggles into me, all warmth and snot. Gross, yes, but she's my little sister so it's sort of cute, too.

"Do you know who that was on the phone?" I ask, hoping to calm her down.

She wipes her running nose on my shoulder. I try not to flinch. "Someone for Mummy. But I told them that Mummy was out."

"Was it my school?" I say. I'm sure it was my school.

"I don't know," she says sadly. "Was Alice outside? Will you let her in?" Fresh tears flood down her fat cheeks.

I sigh, stand up, open the door and shout, "Come in, Alice," to the empty street.

Lauren's face is transformed. "Alice!" she shouts with excitement. "Come and play cafés with me."

And with that, she runs upstairs with her arm outstretched as if she's holding someone's hand.

Yep, you've guessed it. Alice is not real. And the reason that Lauren and Gran don't get on is because Gran thinks that we humor Lauren too much. Which is true. Gran is a big fan of truth. She's the only person in the family who thinks that way. I jump as the phone rings again and, like a trained professional in the art of avoiding unwanted phone calls, I disconnect the phone. Above me, a huge photo of an attractive young woman peers down seductively.

"Hi, Mum," I say.

It's a photo of her in her early twenties, at the height of her so-called modeling career. It's a bit weird looking at it cos you can see a bit of me there — the eyes are the same. But whereas Mum's face is all cheekbones and pout, I look like I've been slightly overinflated by a bicycle pump. How is it that I feel like I'm being judged by my mum and she's not even in the house? Anyway, Mum doesn't do much full-on modeling these days. She's found this niche for herself. You know those close-ups in nail- or hand-moisturizing products? Well, that perfect hand with manicured nails probably belongs to her.

"Having a good day?" I ask Mum. She doesn't answer back. Obvs. Lauren's madness is clearly catching. Assuming that my parents haven't left a four-year-old at home alone, I track down any random adults who might be hiding in the house and may — or may not — have found out about my appalling crimes.

Upstairs, I hear a mobile phone vibrating, knocking into things. Dad's. I peek around the door into his and Mum's bedroom. It's a dangerous activity at any time (my parents still find each other attractive — eek!) but thank God, he's in bed alone, fast asleep. His phone is buzzing like a demented bumblebee, spinning around and round on the shiny surface of the bedside table. He grunts. I grab the phone and turn it off.

He opens an eye. "Whatsgonon?" he mumbles.

"Nothing. You're just dreaming, Dad," I whisper.

He nods and closes his eye again. I despair. Dad should be looking after Lauren, but he's clearly hungover from some gig last night, which means that Gran has been left in charge. Which is a bit tricky cos she never comes out of her attic. The adults in this house leave something to be desired.

In times like these, a girl needs her grandmother. I swear sometimes she's the only sane one in this place, which — given her love of gin — shows the level of dysfunction I live with. I climb the steep wooden steps to the top floor where Gran hangs out. So yes, I do live in quite a posh house. Three levels, nice Victorian floors, original features, etc., but this isn't my parents' house. No, it belongs to Gran. She calls my parents "Fur Coat and No Knickers." I think what she means is that Mum and Dad like look like they're rich but it's all show. My mum calls Gran Saggy Tits, but only when Gran can't hear her.

I knock on her door.

"Come in," she calls with her firm voice. I take a deep breath of clean air and go in and sit next to the open window. It's the only way to keep a clear head when visiting. Gran doesn't smell of wee — but though she's not smoking at the moment, her room does smell of weed.

"Jesobel. Now what might you be doing at home on a school morning?"

See, there's nothing wrong with Gran's brain, despite the constant consumption of illicit drugs. Meanwhile, her son is clearly addled and he's less than half her age.

"I walked out of school," I say bluntly.

Gran nods. "Wise girl. I'm not sure of the need to go every day. All it teaches you is to conform to an authoritarian regime."

I nod.

"Now," she says, "as you're here, you might as well make yourself useful. Scrabble or gin rummy?"

Gran spent most of her life protesting about something. Nuclear power. Fascists. Men who treat women badly. Well, just men, really. And now, she just stays in her attic, listens to Radio 4 and draws. Weird, abstract things, but kind of cool at the same time.

Gran peers at me. "Did something happen?" she purrs. "It's not like you to walk out of school. You appear to be quite the conformist these days."

Ouch. That hurt. There was me thinking I was a bit of a rebel.

"On the surface, Gran," I say, "but today I didn't feel like playing the education game."

"That's my girl," she says. "You only start really learning anything when you leave school. All these exams rot your brain."

This is all normal Gran stuff. She looked after me when I was little, when Dad was still vaguely famous, and Mum and he just cruised around London and the rest of the world. If you think I'm a bit odd, you know, for not starving myself until I'm a stick girl, then she is partly responsible. Just as I'm dealing out the cards, I hear the front door slam.

"Jess!" Mum's voice thunders up the stairs. How can someone so thin make so much noise? "I think it's time we had a little chat."

Her tone of disappointment gets me every time. I mean, this is the woman who puts every ounce of energy, every day, into how she looks. She checks her reflection in any shiny surface that comes her way. Her idea of a blowout is putting a second olive on her microgreens. She was quite a success as a model, and she married a rock star, and she's ended up with me. Mum likes self-help books, but you can't find anything on Amazon along the lines of *I Was a Supermodel — My Daughter's a Whale.*

Gran looks at me. "Well, young lady, it would be rude to keep The Plastic One waiting." She winks. "Come and report back to me later." We exchange grins, but I know I have to leave this sanctuary.

I have to face my fate.

Alone.

CHAPTER SIX

Invisible Rule #5:
When a parent says they want to "talk," it means
they want to tell you off. They talk, you listen.

Mum's voice echoes up the stairs. "Jesobel, I know you're up there."

I expect Dad'll be awake by now. Nothing like the sweet tones of your beloved to bring you back from your dreams. I'm not quite sure what Dad's dreams are but I expect he's on stage somewhere in the early nineties.

As I pass the bedroom, there's definitely movement. A second later, Dad pokes his head around the door, all un-gelled hair and baggy boxers.

"Stephen, get down here and make yourself useful for a change," Mum calls, with more than an edge of acid to her voice.

Dad reappears in some trackies and I can hear him follow me down. Lauren is sitting on the floor outside her room.

"Alice sent me out for answering back. I can go back in when I've spent ten minutes on the naughty step," she says.

I make a mental note to have a chat with Alice later.

But before that, I have to face my mother.

There she stands, fuming. You have to give it to her — she's not let standards slip. From a distance, she looks much the same as she looked twenty years ago. Large-eyed, groomed to perfection, perfect nails sitting on slim hips, she winces as I stomp down the stairs. This is a woman who likes to keep flesh strictly under control.

"Jesobel," she starts, "I've had an interesting phone call from school. Care to tell me what this is about?"

Dad ambles into the living room and I follow. I think I need to sit down, so I throw myself on the sofa. Mum paces, her heels clicking manically on the stripped pine floor.

"So?" she starts. "Shall we begin with what on earth you are wearing?" Her eyes rake down to my bare legs and back up again. "I know you like to make a point about" — she pauses for a second — "your appearance, but I have to say that what you're wearing is unsuitable. I mean, frankly, Jess, I don't want to be harsh but what were you thinking?"

My eyes prick with tears and I stare hard at the floor to keep my face like a mask.

"I mean, if you want advice on which clothes would, well, suit …" Her voice begins to quaver for a moment. "… look good on someone who …"

I let her stumble.

"… chooses to look like you, then you only have to ask. I mean, I do actually know something about fashion."

Dad clears his throat. "Well, I think Jess has the right to express herself through her clothes if that's what she wants to do."

Nice try, Dad, I think, and we exchange smiles. Maybe he isn't so bad after all.

"Let's move on then," Mum says. "I still don't understand why you're sitting at home, half naked, when you should be at school. You start your exams soon and you know how important they are!"

I take a deep breath. "I got into an argument with Zara Lovechild. She pushed me over and I split my leggings."

Mum opens her mouth as if to say something but for once thinks better of it.

"I was going to borrow something to wear but everything kept going wrong. And then Zara was really rude to me and then she sort of fell over. And I might have said some stuff. And then Mrs. Brown saw me and just started screaming at me. Calling me a bully, when *she's* the meanest bully around, but she's a teacher, so you're not allowed to say that. And she wouldn't listen to me so I just had enough." My voice tapers off. Everything I've said sounds so pathetic and childish.

Lauren's voice pipes up. "Mrs. Brown sounds like a knobhead if she's mean to you."

Dad chokes and Mum takes a deep breath. I know she's counting to three and thinking of her happy place like they teach in her self-visualization courses.

"Lauren, sweetie, where did you hear that expression?" Mum asks and she almost sounds calm.

Lauren smiles. "Daddy calls Uncle Barry that all the time when he thinks I'm watching TV. Is a knobhead a nice person or a nasty person, Daddy?"

Dad begins to laugh. Really laugh. And then I giggle. And before you know it, Lauren is squealing on the floor, Dad has tears running down his cheeks and even Mum's taut face cracks a smile (but not across the forehead, cos of the Botox).

Mum is the first to pull herself together. But Dad is the first to speak. "So, Jess told some tight-arsed —"

"Stephen!"

"— some interfering old bully where to go," Dad continues. "And that's it."

"Sort of," I mumble.

"And then she left the school premises," Mum points out. "Jess, you can't just walk out of school. You have to face up to the consequences of your actions. You may have been provoked but you need to show more self-control."

"I'm just sick of school," I say. I wish Gran were here to back me up.

Mum stares at me as if that's not an answer. "Are you okay? Perhaps I should take you to see my doctor. He did wonders for Maria Morrison's youngest."

I say, "I don't need Prozac. I need Zara Lovechild to chill out and teachers not to give me so much stress."

"I really don't see what you have to be stressed about."

I say nothing. Because if I say, *Well, Mum, I find every day a battle against stereotypical ideas of female beauty and an education system that requires you to be "perfect" at all times,* she'll just laugh her tinkly laugh and say, *Being beautiful isn't easy.* So instead I just say, "I don't need a doctor. I just want to be left alone."

"Right on," Dad says. "You don't need doctors messing with your head. Are we nearly done here because I need to get to a rehearsal for you-know-what." He taps his nose like he's in some lame spy film. What he means is that he's doing a gig with all his old bandmates soon and he's treating it like it's a state secret. Which is probably a mistake because unless they actually tell someone, no one will turn up.

Mum sighs. "We all have to go to a meeting tomorrow morning at the school. Nine o'clock with Mr. Ambrose."

Dad starts to protest. "Nine o'clock? That's against my human rights."

She silences him with a glare. "You heard, Stephen. You'll just have to cut your 'rehearsal' short, not roll in at two in the morning after drinking every bar in the area dry." Her laser focus returns to me. "You'll have to apologize." She anticipates what I'm going to say before I even say it. "I know it's not fair, but unfortunately, the world's not fair. I heard what you said, but they say that they've got evidence of you bullying this girl. And the camera never lies."

If my own mum won't back me, then what chance do I have?

Mum sits next to me and puts her thin hand on my plump knee. "You must focus on school. It's not long until your exams, and I don't want to put pressure on you, but you need to do well to get into the best universities."

This from the woman who left school with no qualifications. The only qualifications models need can best be seen in a swimsuit. But I digress. She's still talking.

"I know it's our family tradition that you cook, but all the cook-books, the meals — it's getting a bit out of hand. And your leggings splitting. Don't you think that that might be a sign that perhaps you could think about losing a few pounds? I think you'd be happier if you took care of yourself a bit more."

Mum's voice sounds gentle but I feel the barbs.

"You think I should be like Cat and never eat and just be miserable all the time?"

"Well, no, but as you've brought Cat up, think how well she did in her exams. And she's very popular with boys."

So, that's it. Cat is the daughter of her dreams and I'm just bringing shame on the family? I kind of always knew this but it's hard to hear it.

"So, you think I'll be happier if there is less of me?"

"That's not what I said."

But it's what you meant, I think.

"Why don't you think things over in your room for a bit? You needn't cook tonight. I'll do it." Mum's cooking? So, green salad all round.

"Don't look so sad, Jess," Mum says. "I bought you something while I was out. I left it in your room."

A running machine, I wonder? Or a magic device that sucks fat out? Lauren tries to give me a hug but Mum drags her away and I plod back upstairs to my room, alone.

CHAPTER SEVEN

Observation #3:
If being thin is so great, why are
thin people always miserable?

It's hours before school ends, so I'm on my own until then. How do you fill the time when you're just losing at life in the biggest possible way imaginable?

I could turn my phone back on and see who, if anyone, is concerned about me. But I don't want to see the response to this morning just yet. And anyway, maybe no one cares. So I change into old jeans and a big top (not too revealing for you, Mum?) and I watch TV. Sort of. I've got all of *MasterChef: The Professionals* prerecorded, so I find my favorite episodes, get out my huge "Ideas for Recipes" scrapbook and make notes on any meals I've missed.

A few hours later, I'm hungry and the house seems quiet.

I am unhappy. I consider: What makes me happy when everything is a bit rubbish?

Food. The cooking of it and especially the eating of it.

I'm not sure that's going to work for me today, but I head down to the kitchen. Dad's off being cool somewhere, Mum's taken Lauren

46

shopping probably for her so-called dinner, Gran never leaves her "suite" and Cat's at college. Not that you'd notice if she was here. I open the cupboards and see what there is. After a few minutes of rifling through ingredients and flicking through my books, I have a brainwave. I saw this ultracool thing where someone made the Taj Mahal out of gingerbread. It was an amazing feat of imagination, baking skill and engineering.

For the first time since the whole Zara thing, I properly feel okay. This is my great plan — I'm going to build a model of the school out of gingerbread. And then — this is the best bit — I'm going to eat it. That's tickety — (I stop myself saying that. I sound like a weirdo.) I'm not quite sure what I'm saying here about my feelings about school, but I think it's that school won't get the better of me. I think how satisfying it will be to hear the school walls crunch as I bite down on them.

But it's an epic project, which keeps me busy for the rest of the afternoon. First, I need to plan, and then I need to build.

After three hours of measuring, mixing, baking, cutting and constructing, I stand back and look at my handiwork. The main school bit and then the six portable classrooms that smell in summer and let the rain in in winter. Green icing for the playing fields. And even a little gingerbread clock tower. A bit wonky but definitely a recognizable campanile. It looks fab, even if I do say so myself. I take a photo and leave the gingerbread school there for Mum. She'll have me put in some hospital for crazy people. "Well, Doctor, making buildings out of cake is hardly normal, is it?"

By now it's nearly the end of the school day. Hannah and Izzie will be heading home and I need to talk to them. I don't want to see my family. I want my friends. As far as I'm aware, I'm not under house arrest — I was just told to stay in my room and think things over. Time served and now I'm free. So, I head off out of the house, walk the few streets to Hannah's house, find the key under the third stone from the left flowerpot and let myself in to Hannah's basement, where it all started just a few hours ago. I put on the ancient two-ring stove that we use down here and begin to make hot chocolate for them.

I don't have to wait long.

Hannah and Izzie come through the door exactly 13 minutes and 14 seconds after the school bell would have rung. That is truly a world record — I'm impressed.

They stand there for a minute.

"OMG," Hannah gasps. You know, I'd expect better from someone who reads as much as she does, but clearly it's one of those days where no one does what they're supposed to. "I don't know how you can stand there making hot drinks so calmly."

What is she talking about? Someone could announce the end of the world and I'd say, "Now, who'd like a snack before we all panic?"

Izzie comes and sits next to me on the non-reclining recliner. "Seriously, are you okay?"

"As in, have I gone mad?" I reply. "Not really, I just couldn't help myself. I think I was possessed."

Izzie looks up with interest.

"I was joking. Spirit possession is not the explanation for what happened!" I say before she gets any ideas. "So, what's the word?"

"You've not seen?" Hannah says. "It's all gone crazy. You're all anyone is talking about at school, or at the boys' school. This is better than when that Maths teacher ran away with that boy in Year Ten."

I raise a skeptical eyebrow — it's a look I've perfected over the years. *Seriously?* "I walked out of school. What's the big deal here?"

Izzie and Hannah exchange looks. "You don't know, do you?"

"I don't know what?" I say.

"About the clip?" Hannah replies.

They both start to laugh.

"You will not believe this," Hannah says. She flips up the lid of her ancient laptop.

"How can you not have seen this?"

"I turned my phone off and didn't go on the computer. I wasn't in the mood," I say.

"Well," she says, "I think you'll be in the mood for this. You're everywhere. Look." She's on YouTube. It's a clip called "Fat Girl vs. Mean Girl."

It's me. It's a film of me. And Zara. You see me and my face as she says something that you can't hear. And then you see me say, with added subtitles, what I said: "Grotesque, Zara? That's a big word for you — do you think you can spell it?" And then she lunges forward and I step to the side. She falls flat on her face. And there I am, with my foot on her bum, pretending to be a triumphant boxer. The girls all around are cheering me on.

OMG.

There's a clip of me.

On the Internet.

There have been a few thousand views already.

My first reaction: that's brilliant. My moment of triumph over Zara has been captured forever. Now it's there for all to see.

My second reaction: Do I really look like that?

For once in my life, I am speechless.

I watch the clip over and over again. Partly in disbelief, partly in pride, partly in shock at my legs. I grapple with the knowledge that this clip of me is now being seen all over the world. Maybe girls in Mongolian huts are taking time from milking their yaks to go, "Have you seen that girl on YouTube? She really should lose some weight!"

As I watch, the number of views just goes up and up. I've heard of things going viral but this is beyond weird. Despite my legs being really rather sturdy, they start to wobble and my head spins. I might actually be sick. Weakly, I say, "Who put it on with the subtitles?"

Hannah looks proud. "Oh, that was Sana's idea. We had IT so she just did it then. Do you like it?"

See, normally, I would like it, but now I'm not so sure. I'm beginning to see how the whole world must see me. And the thought that my body is now being broken into squillions of pixels and being sent round the world for people to laugh at is just not okay on any level. Just minutes ago, I was baking in my kitchen and I was in control of me and my ingredients. I'm so not in control of this. A feeling rises up inside me that I'm not quite familiar with. Panic.

Izzie is talking, but I can't hear what she's saying.

"So, have you been expelled?" she says again with excitement.

I shake my head. "I've been suspended for the day and I'm in with the parents for the appointment of doom at nine o'clock."

I sigh. We all sigh. We all know that this will not be fun.

But that was before the clip. Which could change things. It's one thing to break the school rules. It's another thing to be seen to break school rules by the whole world.

Izzie pipes up, "Do you want me to read your tarot cards?"

I bite my tongue (a bit). "You know, I'm gonna give that a miss today."

Hannah changes tack. "Let's log on. You've got to see this." She knows my password and, seconds later, there's my Instagram account. It's mad — loads of messages from people I've never heard of. Or people who have been too cool to know me in the past.

Hannah says, "You need to think before you say anything, cos people are gonna want something special from you."

Obvs!

"So, my latest recipe for bouillabaisse isn't gonna cut it?" I say.

Izzie gives me a withering look. "Your obsession with food is just as weird as my interest in magic."

"Except food is real and essential for life," I say.

Then I remember the gingerbread model of the school. That is exactly what this moment needs.

Seconds later, I've posted the photo. Underneath I've put: If you don't like something, eat it. #thegirlwhoeatslife

Izzie looks confused. "What does that even mean?"

"I don't know — I just thought it sounded good. What else am I supposed to say? Hannah, words of wisdom?" I'm really hoping Hannah will come through for me here because I have all these feelings and no words to express them. If I *could* eat life, I would.

"Sorry," Hannah says. "Strangely enough, Jane Austen doesn't always have wise words to say on how to survive in a multimedia world ..."

At this moment, there is a knock on the door. The inside door, not the outside one that everyone uses. No one uses the inside door except Hannah, and she's sitting here with us. Hannah's family never comes down — that's why we like it here.

We look at each other. Hannah yells, "Come in!"

Through the door comes Hannah's brother Alex and, with him — pinch yourselves cos it's true — Matt Paige. Yes, that Matt Paige, the one I have a huge and secret crush on, the Matt Paige who's in my head every night as I go to sleep. The one I've been on numerous dates with, the one I've kissed, gotten married to and had three children with (all girls, if you're interested). But also the Matt Paige who I've never actually spoken to before. Never been closer than twenty feet to before. And here he is. If I reached out, I could almost touch his thigh. I really, really want to touch his thigh.

"Hi," says Alex.

"Hi," says Matt.

"Hi," I say, trying to look cool, but suddenly I'm aware that I'm running a temperature of 104 degrees, and my heart has decided to do a drum and bass rhythm with a dubstep vibe. I sit on my hand so I don't do anything really stupid like touch him without meaning to. I think I might start giggling. All this emotion and all anyone has said is *hi*. Who says romance is dead?

He's just a boy.

But he is lovely. I could just lie down at his feet and tell him I love him.

Did I actually think that? Have I just broken every rule I hold dear, for a BOY? It's a good job Gran's not dead, or she'd be turning in her grave to hear me talk like this.

So, I pull myself together — I will not be so pathetic! I smile a bit to look friendly, but not enough to show how much I like him. I end up grimacing like a constipated baboon. A badly dressed, constipated baboon because now I'm horribly aware that I threw these clothes on to be comfy. Why did I leave the house like this? I mean, clothes are important, right?

"So, Jess," Alex says, "what exactly have you been up to?"

I've known Alex since I was six. He's skinny and a bit ginger. Whereas Hannah looks like some kind of artist's model, Alex looks like a slightly more attractive Ron Weasley. I think I can speak to him without my voice wavering several octaves.

"Oh, you know, the usual," I say, aiming to sound bored. "Attendance, two altercations with Zara Lovechild, getting into a confrontation with a teacher," I say. "Oh yes, and becoming a YouTube sensation. Nothing special." That was a great humblebrag, I tell myself. Ten out of ten, there, for cool.

I'm not so cool the moment I realize that Matt's burnt-caramel eyes are locked on me. It's like I'm the cupcake and he's about to eat me. Suddenly, I feel incredibly hot. And very, very visible.

"That was quite a lot of sass for one day," Matt says.

Sass? Is that good? Is that bad? What does he mean by that? I will have to analyze every possible interpretation later — I don't have time now.

"I think you'll find I'm the queen of sass, generally." I just about manage to keep eye contact without dying.

He's still looking and still smiling. "Queen of sass? I like it. I thought you were queen of cakes."

I'm taking this all in my stride. "I can be queen of both, you know. Next cake, I'll combine both my talents and I'll bake the sassiest thing you've ever eaten." Hannah is looking at me with her mouth half open, which is fair enough, cos what does that even mean? I have metaphorically just tripped over my tongue. I am an idiot.

"So what actually happened? What did the lovely Zara do to make you so angry?" Matt asks, his hair falling down over his eyes. It's only the Zara comment that stops me from sweeping his hair back from his forehead.

"Zara isn't so lovely to me, I'm afraid. She committed the worst crime of all — she said I couldn't bake." No need to mention that the fight was all about her calling me fat. Now is not the time to draw attention to that.

"Zara is such a cow," Alex says with surprising anger.

"Cheers, mate," I say. "I'll make you some of your favorite brownies if you like."

"You can make brownies?" Matt says. Like I am some sort of genius.

"Only sassy ones," I reply. I am on fire today. I'm beginning to enjoy myself. And I rather think from the way he's staring back at me that he's enjoying himself, too.

"Jess should be on TV," Alex says with pride. "Have you seen this?" He pulls out his phone and shows Matt a photo of my gingerbread school. How has he seen that already? I've only just posted it.

I'm just about to ask him when Matt looks at it and looks at me. "You did that?" he asks.

I blush. "I was bored," I say.

"The girl who eats life? Cool." I think I might melt under the weight of his approval.

"Look at the detail," says Izzie.

"Yeah, I see it," Matt says. He smiles at me still.

I allow myself a small smile back.

"You're Cat Jones's little sister then?" he continues.

I wait a second for him to make some comment about not believing that we're sisters or that I'm not in fact that little at all. He doesn't do either. Score!

"You can tell by your eyes." He noticed my *eyes* (and I think that they are quite nice, actually).

"The name's Jesobel," I say. "Jess for short."

"You should just go by Jesobel," Matt says. He says my name slowly so the *s* sound drags out forever like a kiss. "It's a cool name. No one would ever forget a Jesobel."

"I like to think I'm unforgettable by any name." Hannah is giving me a death stare. Too much? I change the subject. "Cat is short for Caterina but you're not supposed to know that. She's going out with Jack Armstrong from your school," I drop in.

Alex and Matt exchange glances.

"What?" says Izzie. "Is he up to something?"

Matt shrugs. "No ... He does seem to hang out with his ex a lot. But then, that's not a crime."

Alex changes the subject. "Good work there — you did well with Zara and the infamous Mrs. Brown, but she's gonna want your head on a spike. Come on, Matt, we need to practice. The band's waiting."

"Oh, I didn't know you'd joined the band," I find myself saying. "What kind of music are you into?"

"Mostly guitar stuff from the nineties. I'm a big fan of your dad's, actually," Matt answers.

A light bulb goes over my head.

I have never thought that having a dad like mine was much use. It might sound glamorous, but the reality is he's hardly around. All of a sudden, I see an opportunity opening up in front of me.

Alex says, "You know, you could come and listen to us rehearse if you like."

"I'd like that very much." I'm about to jump up and follow them out the door, but I find a firm hand on my arm and a voice saying, "Thanks, but we've got stuff to do."

The tone of Hannah's voice means that I mustn't argue back, for reasons I don't understand. The guys start to go, but Matt stops in the doorway and turns. "My parents are going away in a few weeks' time, so of course, while it's predictable, it has to be done. I'm having a few friends over. You wanna come?" He smiles and takes us all in: the fat girl, the bookworm and the witch. "I mean all of you. I want a house full of people."

"Great," I croak. "We'll check our diaries."

"Just make sure you're there," Matt says as he stands in the door, framed by light. "I'll be looking out for you, Jesobel Jones."

The door shuts and he's gone. Anxiety drains away, but so does the buzz that's been making my brain and body blaze.

I recline on the non-reclining recliner. My heart really is going to pop this time. I want to be independent, mature, follow my own path. But then the second this guy, this one guy, talks to me, it's like I'm going to explode.

Izzie mutters, "Not sure that I want to go."

Hannah stares at her. "Well, *you* might not want to but a certain somebody does!"

Izzie's head does a tennis swivel from me to Hannah. "What, have I just missed something?"

"Only the most enormous amount of sexual tension," Hannah says.

Izzie looks closely at me. "You fancy Alex?" Her voice goes all strange and wavery at the end.

I spit out my hot chocolate. "No," I say.

"Okay, keep your hair on," she says. "Well, that leaves Matt."

"Yes," says Hannah, "it does."

And they both look at me.

That secret crush that I would die before revealing? Seems it's not so secret now.

CHAPTER EIGHT

Invisible Rule #6:
In this enlightened age, girls are still not allowed to ask
guys out. You have to wait for them to make a move. Otherwise
you're "pushy." Or "easy." Either way, it's not cool.

I sigh. Time for the truth to come out. "I just think he seems nice."

Nice seems a very bland word for all the emotions that swept through me a few minutes ago. I mean, my heart is only just returning to a normal beat. In fact, I'm not even sure that my heart is still inside me. I think it's following Matt up the stairs into the house, whimpering like a lonely puppy.

I try to pull myself together.

"Hannah, surely you realized before — I asked you all those questions about him."

Hannah shakes her head. I really don't like this silence. I mean, we do talk about boys all the time. Which ones are okay, which ones are not. But it is a bit of a touchy subject as Hannah was going out with Lucas Harrison for three months until he started giving her grief for not sleeping with him.

So she did.

And then he dumped her anyway.

So, you know, it's easier sometimes just to ask her about what she's reading.

I've kissed and been kissed. I mean, I go to parties. At the end of the evening, you can normally find someone who's not paired off and is happy to snog (and the rest) for a while. Dom and I had a thing for a bit where we tried stuff out on each other. But I've not really had a boyfriend. Not a proper public one. I don't know if it's Gran's influence or too many silly rom-coms.

"Is he unbelievably out of my league?" I ask.

They look long and hard at each other.

Ouch. These are good friends. Hannah starts slowly. "His last girl-friend was … a bit different from you."

I nod. This could be helpful. I don't know any of this. "So, two things, a) is he single now? and b) how was she different?"

Hannah takes her time on this one. "She was … high maintenance."

"You mean she was difficult, or she took great care of herself?"

Izzie chips in here. "I saw them in Starbucks sometimes. She ordered extra hot, skinny macchiatos, easy on the syrup. And then she only drank half. I'd say both."

I swallow. I have to say this and I have to hear their answer. "So she's prettier than me, thinner than me and better dressed than me. And knows when to stop eating." This is why Hannah held me back. She thought that I'd be making a fool of myself if I showed any interest. Matt's too hot for a fat girl like me.

Izzie and Hannah shrug and a painful silence grows.

Hannah tells me the truth. "Yes, she's thinner than you. But, Jess, you've always said you don't care about that. You're pretty, she's pretty. You don't care about fashion, really, and she does."

"I know what I've said," I say. "But I do care about clothes. I just find them difficult. I mean, shop girls give me the evil eye every time

I walk in. And do you want to try going to the back of the store every time, because they put all the smaller sizes up front?"

Hannah moves toward the little stove. "Time for more hot chocolates, I think."

Things are that bad then.

I just wanted to believe that I had a chance with him.

We drink our hot chocolates in a rare awkward silence. All I think about is how I looked in the YouTube clip. Fat. Yes, I had attitude and I'm sure I could find other positives if I thought about it. But my mind is just fixed on one thought. All of a sudden, my hot chocolate tastes far too sickly and sweet.

"I'm off," I mutter, putting down my unfinished drink.

Hannah looks at me with surprise. "Are you okay? You're not worried about this, are you?"

I smile a big, fake smile. "'Course not. What have I got to worry about?" Not like I've got a meeting with the Head, my mum's furious with me and I'm too fat for leggings and too fat for Matt. "See you tomorrow."

Ever-faithful Izzie says, "I'll message you later."

I nod and dodge out through the door. But where do I go? I don't want to go home. So I drift down the street, trying to make sense of all the thoughts that fizz through my mind. Part of my mind is cheering: you had a conversation with Matt. He invited you to a party. The world has seen that Zara is a bully. But the drumbeat underneath those thoughts goes *Fat. Fat. Fat.* I find a bench next to a small patch of grass surrounded by trees. It's not such an awful place to sit, so I slump down and stare at the leaves in the sunlight. Anything to stop thinking about everything else. I sit there for a very long time and the shadows of the trees start to lengthen. If I stay a bit longer, maybe ivy will grow around me, and I'll just have to stay here and become one with nature. Then a small dog runs past me, and I realize that every dog in the neighborhood will wee on me.

As I sit there, pondering whether I am actually capable of movement, or whether I should just wait until a dog gets suspiciously close, he walks past.

Yes. Him. Matt.

I've only spoken to him once in real life, and here he is again.

For a moment, I just enjoy watching him. He sort of slouches along with his shoulders bunched, as if to walk at his full height might give him an unfair advantage over the world. He's so lovely. Do I let him walk by? Do I call him over? Why would I do that, given that I've just been told by my friends that he's far too hot for me.

So I just let him walk on. If you love something, let it go. Or something like that.

But then something happens that is equally magical and terrifying. Matt sees me and smiles what appears to be a genuine smile. I find myself grinning at him like an idiot as he crosses the road and throws himself down next to me on the bench. He's sitting right beside me. Maybe six inches apart? Does that mean he likes me? My brain cannot cope with this calculation. He crossed a road to be with me, risking life and limb. Have you seen how badly rich people drive in their huge black SUVs round here? He could have been killed. My friends were wrong — we are destined to be together.

But destiny or not, my brain is letting me down. There are words buzzing round my head but none of them seem to make any sense. He's not saying anything either. Who comes over to a girl and then says nothing? It's not as if my very beauty has struck him dumb.

Eventually, I manage, "How did band practice go?" Lame but at least it's words.

"Okay," he says. "Alex's got homework so we had to finish early. God, that boy's a nerd. But we've got a gig coming up. And, in fact, we've just been booked to play at your Leavers' Ball. Your pal Zara organized it." Then he winks at me. What does a wink mean? I think desperately. Is that a sign of flirtation? Maybe he's just got something in his eye.

"The ball. How cool," I find myself gushing.

And then there's a silence. I don't want a silence. I'm scared of silence. Silence means we're not compatible. Silence means he's going to walk away from me and then I won't feel that glorious energy that buzzed through me when we were talking before.

My poor brain twists itself in knots. Then I remember. He said he liked my dad's music. That's my way in. "My dad's first-ever gig was at the Scout hut, down the road, you know. He was about twelve at the time."

"Twelve? Really?" A raised eyebrow tells me he doesn't believe me.

"Really. He wore sunglasses all the time and his collar turned up to hide how young he was."

Matt's giving me his full megawatt stare. "So that's how his look started?"

I nod, beginning to feel much more confident. "All about hiding how young he was. And he just stuck with it. All these years."

"His playing was immense. Probably the best thing about the band. What's it like to have a rock star for a dad?" he continues.

"He's not really a rock star. More of a rock twinkle, really," I say, thinking of how useless Dad is at anything dad-like. "When Cat goes out dressed in a few wisps of material, he doesn't yell, 'I've seen hand-kerchiefs bigger than that. No daughter of mine is going out like that.' Instead, he'll just go, 'Cool.'"

Matt appears to be laughing. "Rock twinkle. I like it. Maybe that's my life ambition right there."

I glow in the moment. Maybe I am too fat for him to like me, but at this precise moment, he seems to be enjoying my company and I am going to savor every minute.

"He's not the only eccentric in the family. You should meet my baby sister. She's bullied by her imaginary friend." Now Matt's brow crinkles as he tries to process that one. "Weird? I know," I continue. "And then there's Gran. How many grandmothers do you know who live mostly on gin and illegal drugs?"

I am totally giving Matt's face a workout because now his jaw has dropped. "Not really?"

"Really." Is this becoming a thing? Like one of those cute things that couples do — one of us says, "Really?" and then the other repeats it. We'll do this on our wedding day and everyone will laugh and say, "How cute!"

"But she can't survive like that."

I nod with grim satisfaction. "She was last seen eating a nut cutlet in 2012. She nearly choked and swore never to eat again as it was too dangerous. She swore only to consume gin from then on as she says it's safer. You can't choke on it." This is almost true.

He's properly laughing now, and the most glorious warm glow fills me from top to bottom. Like when you eat warm bread fresh from the oven. I can make Matt laugh. It's like we were meant to be together.

"Okay, you do have a weird family. Maybe I should drop around and meet them sometime?" Is that like a date? He's making intense eye contact with me. I think I might be having a heart attack. Why is he acting like this, like he might really like me? I'm so confused.

But then his phone buzzes and drags his attention away. It's like there was a spotlight on me that's now switched off. I am silent while he scans his message.

"Got to go, I'm afraid." He flashes a quick, glorious smile at me. What can I say or do to make him stay?

"Dad's playing a gig next week," I find myself saying. "It's supposed to be a secret, but he's going to be playing with the old lineup for one night only."

I feel the full heat of the spotlight back on me as puts his phone down and looks at me.

"A secret reunion?" he asks.

"Just a bunch of middle-aged guys rocking out," I say modestly.

"And you can get tickets?"

Can I get tickets? I've never asked before. But I'm the daughter of the guitarist, so surely I can get tickets.

"Absolutely. Do you want to come?"

"I wouldn't miss it for the world. Gotta go. History essay calls. But give me your number." He stabs it into his phone. "I'll be in touch. Make sure you come to my party, Cat's Little Sister."

"The name's Jesobel," I say.

"The girl who eats life. I know."

And there you are. The best moment of my life so far. Just as I'm mulling over my clever retort, he leaps to his feet and slouches off into the distance without so much as a backward glance.

So, I need to get tickets for the gig. Shouldn't be that hard. But I do desperately need the answer to this question: Is it a date?

CHAPTER NINE

Observation #23:
Life is generally easier if you conform.
But it is also duller.

I'm not sure how long I sit there in a happy bubble. He talked to me. He liked me. He said he wanted to meet my family. But then other thoughts crowd in to spoil the party. I still look the way I do and he still looks the way he does. Maybe I can find out his favorite food and feed him up so we match.

Why am I doing this to myself? Part of me knows I'm setting myself up for failure, but I can't help the way I feel when he's around. Plus, imagine Zara's face if Matt went out with me. Imagine Mum's face if Matt went out with me! That would be a way to show them I'm not such a waste of space.

My phone buzzes to distract me and stops me melting like butter. Dinner is ready. Thank God Mum is too lazy to walk upstairs to tell me this, so I've got just enough time to run home. I think I'm grounded. The fact that no one has noticed I'm not even home tells you all you need to know about my family.

I slip in the side door and look for my gingerbread school, just to make me feel better, but it's gone. All that's left are a few gingery crumbs. Was it all too mad for Mum? Did she throw the rest out? But even worse than that — guess who's sitting in my kitchen, big sweating hands pawing over my sister? Yep, it's Jack, Cat's boyfriend. Problem is that IMHO he's an A-plus asshat. Whatever I want from me and Matt, this is not it.

Picture the scene. Cat slouches, unsmiling (i.e., in her default position), at the table. Jack has his arm around her, slowly stroking her shoulder with small possessive movements, but his eyes are welded on my mum's bum as she bends over, getting something out of the oven. I stand in the doorway for a second, observing it all.

Jack's eyes flicker over to me. He knows that I've seen him staring at Mum's bum but he clearly thinks it's funny. Cat appears oblivious. Will she ever speak again? I suppose I don't really want to know the answer to this, but what do each of them get out of this relationship? I suppose they look good together, like some kind of god-awful perfume advert.

As Mum struggles with the weight of the tray she's pulling from the oven, Jack leaps up.

"Let me help," he purrs as he takes it from her and puts it safely on the table. "Smells delicious, Mrs. Jones," he says.

"Call me Annabel, please, Jack. You make me feel so old, and after all, I'm not married," Mum says. "Rock stars don't get married." Save me. That's worthy of an eye roll, surely.

But said eye roll means Mum sees me. For a moment, I think there's going to be a rerun of this morning, but clearly she doesn't want a row in front of Jack, so she fixes a blank smile on her face. "Oh, darling," she says, "I was wondering where you were." So she's not seen the clip yet. "Well, I've done some chicken for tea. There's salad on the table. Dad's gone out so it's just the four of us. Lauren's gone to play at a friend's house."

"I'll be Daddy then, shall I?" Jack says. He winks at Mum, who blushes slightly.

Is this just me or is it a bit weird? Cat is intent on her phone. She reads something and narrows her eyes for just a second. Jack reaches over, takes the phone from her hand and turns it off.

Right. You don't mess with someone's phone. That's just not on. I watch Cat to see if she'll do anything. Cat looks at him. He smiles back. If it were me, I'd smack him.

I look to Mum to see if she's picking up on his passive-aggressive tendencies, but she just beams again. "Good idea, Jack. Nice to have you with us, Cat."

My beautiful sister is as silent and impassive as ever. But she reaches over Jack, snatches the phone, switches it on and puts it carefully back on the table next to her. Jack laughs, but there is no warmth in his eyes. Cat–1, Idiot Boyfriend–0. I think of Matt leaning back in the late afternoon sun, laughing at my family stories. He would never be like this, surely. No perving on Mum. No stealing of phones. I have to believe that it's possible to find a boy who wants to go out with you and will treat you like a human being, not an accessory. Cat's and my eyes meet just for a second before her eyes slide away, the smallest ghost of a smile on her lips. Is this a rare moment of solidarity?

As Mum dishes out the chicken breasts, I look critically at her work. "They're more tender if you cook them with the skin on," I start.

"Too many calories," Mum says bluntly. "Have some salad."

I look around for the salad dressing but can't see any, so I walk over to the larder to get the oil, vinegar and mustard. As I whip them up, I watch my mum and sister at work at the table.

Mum piles a huge amount of green salad next to her chicken. Carefully, she goes through the leaves and puts every single olive back into the salad bowl. What's the point of making a salad with olives if you're going to take them all out again?

Cat regards her chicken carefully. Cuts it in half. And then in half again. Puts three quarters of it back and then cuts the remainder into tiny baby-sized mouthfuls. Very deliberately, she chews each mouthful twenty times and drinks between each one. Yes, Cat eats like she's a celebrity.

I return to the table with my freshly made and particularly well-seasoned dressing. I've added a bit of fresh tarragon to bring out the flavor of the chicken and the tomato. After pouring it liberally over my meal, I offer the jug to Mum and Cat. Both wave it away, but I see Mum's hand edge toward it when she thinks I'm not looking. I bite into the salad and savor the rich taste of the dressing. "You don't know what you're missing."

"Better go easy on that, Jess," Jack says. He smiles at me like a shark.

"Are you calling me fat?" I return, deciding to go for direct confrontation.

Jack goes into super-smooth mode. "'Course not, Jess. Curves are all the rage, right?"

C'mon, Jess, say something good. I need a moment to think this through and, while doing so, I enjoy my chicken. Never start a verbal assault with a full mouth of food. I remember what I posted earlier. If you don't like something, eat it.

"I was talking to Matt and Alex today, Jack," I say.

I choose my words carefully. I don't want to upset my sister.

"They said you hang out with them sometimes. They told me who else you hang out with, too."

My words hang in the air. Have I said too much or not enough?

Jack glares, Cat stares. The two of them then exchange a glance. Cat's eyes are full of anger. At him. At me. Whatever that moment was between us, I've managed to obliterate it.

Cat stops, with most of her small portion left to go. "Thanks, Mum," she says and pushes her food away. Jack pushes his plate toward me. "Want to finish off my seconds?" he says with a glint in his eyes.

"Not my style," I return. At least not in front of him.

I'd like to think that that's Jess–1, Asshat–0. But somehow I'm not that sure. I mean, first of all, I've been a bit mean. And then, as Cat and Jack leave, she puts her hand in his and then he smiles back as if she's the most beautiful thing he's ever seen. He strokes away a stray hair from her face and kisses her on the forehead. They seem lost in their own little world. Like a happy couple.

What would I give — what would I do — to get Matt to look at me like that?

CHAPTER TEN

Observation #4:
The Internet is great for cheating on your
homework (sorry, for "independent research"),
but it's also just another way to fail at life.

I head up to my room to sort out the mess of feelings that are swirling around inside me like a psychedelic kaleidoscope. Maybe I should try one of Gran's "herbal" cigarettes. Or then again not.

I try to recap the day:

1. It felt cool to get one over on Zara.

2. It felt great to walk away from Mrs. Brown. That was amazing and possibly my finest moment on this planet to date. For a few seconds, I was the person that I wanted to be — no compromise, no regrets.

3. Even better and weirder — those cool moments are now on the Internet and people might be watching all over the world. (Downer that they'll see my legs, but let's just gloss over that for now.)

4. And then the highest high — Matt Paige has found out who I am.

5. He has looked straight in my eyes and not laughed or puked or made any joking reference to my size. Like he didn't even notice.

6. He has asked me to his party.

7. He has asked for my number and agreed to go to a gig with me.

This is all amazingly amazing. Even tickety-boo.

But still, despite that connection I feel every time he looks at me, there's something not quite right. Is it fear? Matt has been my secret fantasy crush for a year now. If I get to know him better, will he be a letdown? I'm in control of my daydreams, so fantasy Matt will never let me down. But real Matt could end up like Jack, for all I know — be a bit of an idiot. But apart from that fear, there's certainly a dash of hope. More than a healthy feeling of excitement. And there we go again, there's a bit more fear. Fear of making a fool of myself. Matt might let me down gently, but if Zara ever heard about it, she would make my life a misery.

As I pace round the room, I see a long parcel draped over the chair. The color of the wrapping makes me think it's from one of the few shops that designs clothes I really like.

Maybe it's a peace offering from Mum. She did mention that she'd bought something for me earlier. And I have to admit that she does have great taste. I rip off the packaging and hold up the contents so that I can see it properly.

It's a dress, and it's perfect.

I put it up to my face — the color, soft blue, is exquisite. It's low cut enough to suggest my boobs without being blatant, shaped for curves, still good over jeans or leggings — sexy but cool. I have to hand it to her. My mum does know something about fashion.

Then a thought strikes me.

I check the label.

I feel like being sick.

How could she?

It's one size too small.

Maybe it was a mistake. Maybe she just subconsciously bought the dress size she'd rather I be. Or is this a gentle nudge to get me to shift some pounds? It doesn't feel like a gentle nudge. It feels like a kick in the stomach.

I'm clearly in the mood to torture myself so I strip down to bra and pants and put it on.

The dress may be perfect but I am not.

I look at myself in the mirror.

In the mirror, a fat girl stands, her eyes holes of misery in her face. Her boobs stretch the fabric, her stomach looks enormous and the material shines over her bum. The zip is stuck halfway.

I know what Mum would say. *If you'd just put a bit of effort in, in a few weeks, you'd look a million dollars.*

I would like to look in a mirror and be happy. I was this morning.

So if I don't like what I see, then perhaps I should … eat less? I think about Hannah and Izzie this morning and I think about #thegirlwhoeatslife. How confident I was about it earlier today. How I teased them, so confident that I was right. And yet, here I am, agreeing with Mum and Zara, even Cat.

I want to wear this to Matt's party. Could I have the dress changed to make it larger? Or — and this is when the big thought crashes in — do I have to change to fit into the dress?

I take it off and just hold its softness to my face.

The dress says, *Just try for a few days and see how it goes.*

The dress says, *No pressure, no compromise.*

The dress says, *Find nice food that is lower in calories. Look at the saturated fat content. Hell, would it kill you to do some exercise?*

The dress says, *Just give it three weeks.*

How many corny movies have I seen where the geeky girl is transformed into some kind of goddess and then gets the guy? He looks at her in a new way, like boys look at Cat, like Matt looked at me ... once. Hannah and Izzie told me that Matt was out of my league. But why? You don't agree to go to see a gig with a girl if you can't bear to be near her. You don't invite a girl to a party unless you like her company. In my head, I replay my favorite daydreams with Matt. I cook him my favorite dishes and we taste the food together. We walk hand in hand through the park after he's waited for me after school, so all the world can see that he's my guy and we're together.

Deep breath time. How much do I want things to work between me and Matt? What would I be prepared to do to have a real shot with him?

I look at the dress, so soft and feminine. I look at me in my bra and pants. I keep looking, trying to find something positive to say to myself. But all I can see is image after image of thin girls from Instagram, adverts and fashion shoots. None of them look like me.

Right, I tell myself, stop feeling so sorry for yourself. You're just going to make a few lifestyle adjustments. You can change your mind at any point.

I imagine myself turning up to the party, looking stunning. Matt can't take his eyes off me. Is it worth it? Is he worth it? I don't know. But I know I want to try and find out.

After pulling on my pajamas, I make my way down to the kitchen with an empty feeling inside me. It's dark and quiet downstairs. This feels all wrong. Normally, when I'm cooking, it's all out in public for everyone to enjoy. This feels like I'm ashamed.

The kitchen is in shadow, and when I open the fridge, butter-yellow light falls across the black tiles. I don't really need to look inside cos I know every item in there.

I take out the box of cupcakes left over from this morning.

I start to eat one. It's as glorious as ever, so sweet, light and fluffy. But halfway through, I stop.

I smell its light sponge, give it a little kiss and then put it back. I've made my choice. I can't be the girl who eats life. I can't be the girl who eats at all. I want to be the girl who can look in a mirror and smile again. I want to be the girl with the boy on her arm.

Goodbye, cupcake. Goodbye, Old Jess.

For now.

CHAPTER ELEVEN

Invisible Rule #8:
Guys can't wear pink. Or wear skirts. Or glitter.
Which makes some of them sad, I think.
Pink's just a color, isn't it?

I didn't sleep well last night.

Here are just a few reasons:

1. I appear to have become a viral meme. My phone is actually going to burst with notifications.

2. I have a meeting with the Head and my parents this morning.

3. Matt Paige looked at me.

4. I need to think of a way to get my own back on Zara.

5. I have the most important exams of my life in few weeks. College, jobs, future existence — all rest on getting those top grades. If only I could cook a lovely meal instead and get judged on that.

6. I, Jesobel Jones, have decided to go on a new eating regime even though I have always laughed at those who do this. I have sold out.

And now I'm awake and I don't see much chance of going back to sleep, given the incredibly loud noise from outside.

Bloody birds. It's early spring and all they can do at five a.m. is tweet. Don't they have phones for that? Mother Nature needs to catch up PDQ and get them on the real Twitter, and Western Europe will sleep a lot better. (Am I making any sense? Clearly, the idea of eating less has tipped me over the edge.)

So, I think, this is the first day of a new me. So far, so good. I've been awake for ten minutes and I've not eaten anything. Way to go, me.

I think over my general understanding of losing weight.

1. I need to burn more calories than I eat.

2. So less is good. The less I eat, the more I'll lose. (Some disagree on this, but I don't see how you can eat lots of food and still lose weight. There are, however, lots of things in the world that I don't understand: the Higgs boson particle, patterned leggings, why anyone watches sports ...) Celebrities seem to go on weird diets where they eat nothing but cabbage or maple syrup. The last one seems to make more sense but the first one sounds like a disaster. Okay, you might be skinny but your farts would kill off any living organisms standing next to you. Skinny but lonely would be the end result and what's the use of that?

3. Fruit and veg are best, I think, but beyond that, it gets all confusing. Good carbs, bad carbs, good fats, bad fats ...

weird diets with even weirder names. I could spend a lifetime on Google researching this but I think I'll just stick with number 1.

So here I am, on zero calories. If I do some exercise, then I'll be in minus calories, and then I can eat something (salady) later in the day. This seems like a plan. I'm too wired to sleep and the streets should be quite quiet at this hour of the morning. Mum won't be too stoked to find me running around the neighborhood on my own, but then surely all would be forgiven when she finds out why. And after all, I've got my phone — my adult-to-child tracker device — so what can possibly go wrong?

What to wear? Never my strong point. Obvs, the main idea is sweats and trainers — even I can work that out. But it's the underwear that's troubling me. I swim, I go to the gym sometimes, but I've never actually run any distance. And the main reason for that is my boobs.

Apparently, constructing a bra is one of the most difficult engineering tasks known to humankind. You have to make a structure that's comfortable to wear and can accommodate two unsupported blobs of jelly that can move up, down, sideways and any variation in between. I rummage through my drawers to see what I can do about this. Oh, yes, and it should be vaguely attractive — i.e., not something Gran would wear. Actually, Gran doesn't bother with a bra anymore. Which is a bit scary.

Fortunately, whatever failings my mum has, she is very fussy about my bras, and so, as I pull out one elastic garment after the other, I find that I am the proud owner of three sports bras. Well, I think, three should do the trick.

So without any further mucking about, I put them on. All of them. I jump up and down gently just to test them out. Solid as a rock. Two large boobs, firmly strapped in place. After pulling on an old hoodie and trackies, I look at myself in the mirror. Something peculiar has happened to my boobs. They appear to have been relocated just beneath each armpit.

I squeak down the stairs. There are snuffles from various bedrooms, but no one leaps out at me and asks what I'm doing. Within seconds, I've unlocked the front door, carefully pushed it back, waited for a few seconds so Mum can come rushing down to demand what I'm up to.

Nothing. I've made it outside.

I'm vaguely disappointed.

Now what?

Apart from the birds, there's not much going on. No one on the streets, very few lights on in dark houses, a solitary car slowly going past. Over the dark roofs, the pale blue sky is streaked with wisps of pink gold. Look at me — no breakfast is making me all poetic. I'll be writing sonnets and turning into an emo before you know what's happening. Shaking off such ideas, I take a deep breath, open the front gate and then put one foot in front of the other. That's running, isn't it? I repeat the process, only more quickly this time, and off I go.

I'm doing okay — I've reached the end of the road and I've not died. The air feels harsh in my lungs and I'm getting hotter, but apart from that, I'm okay, honestly. Boobs are staying where they should be, feet don't hurt. Lungs are working and I do a bit of Biology review, picturing in my head a multicolor dissection of my lungs with blue and red lines to show oxygenated blood going out and deoxygenated blood coming in. Sorted — the A-plus will be mine! By now, end of the next road, my breath is coming thick and fast and my chest is starting to hurt. I head toward the park — I can do a few laps there, and then think about heading for home. Half an hour, steady pace, no food until lunchtime — easy-peasy lemon-squeezy.

In the distance, I see two figures running toward me on the opposite pavement. All of a sudden, I think about who they might be. There's a strong possibility that they are SOWs, that they'll know my mum and tell her all about my early morning running.

I suppose it doesn't matter if anyone sees me but I pull my hood over my face and continue. Truth is, would anyone recognize me anyway? Surely my face has now swollen up into some alien mask that bears little resemblance to me and more to something jumping out at you in the dark.

The two skinny figures get closer, and the slightly smaller one, though running at pace, is still managing to talk at great length, volume and speed. It's a voice that I recognize, with a peculiarly nasal quality and piercing tone. They're only feet from me and they don't seem to have noticed me, but I'll bet you a brioche that it's Zara Lovechild.

For a second, heat blazes through my mind, confusing my thought processes. They run nearer me, I slowly come nearer to them. Any second now, Zara will see me. She will know that I have caved in.

A space opens out on my left. There's a low hedge that backs on to the bowling green. Panic takes over me.

I jump over the hedge and fall flat on my back. I hold my breath. I hear Zara's voice whinge on about how much studying she's done. Her voice is over my head. She just needs to look down and there I'll be: laid out at her tiny feet like some kind of a sacrifice at the plastic altar of meanness. Yesterday, I had my foot on her bum, but I get a feeling that she's winning now.

"Zara, darling, Chloe Simcock's daughter got eleven A-pluses, so I don't see why you can't," I hear the other person say. I wonder if this is the she-wolf mother I've heard about.

"Mummy, I can't — that's just unfair."

"Eleven A-pluses and you can have the nose job. That's the deal."

They're over me, past me and then they run on.

Nose job? In return for A-pluses? Even for round here, home of football players and their model wives, that's a bit messed up. I can't believe that I'm even thinking this, but here we go anyway.

Poor Zara. I mean — yes, she's a cow. But even my mother would never go that far.

I can't lie on the ground all day. I'm starting to worry I've leaped in some dog poo. I peer over the low hedge — no one near.

It's only when I'm standing up that I see that Zara and her plastic mother haven't run on. Oh no — they're doing some yoga stretches over on the grass.

I stand, frozen. *Don't look this way. Just don't.*

Then Zara looks. She takes in my messy hair, my sportswear, my three bras.

She knows why I'm here. A smug smile creeps over her perfect face. I don't feel sorry for her anymore.

There's no doubt about the score now.

Skinny People–1, Jess–0.

I limp home.

CHAPTER
TWELVE

Invisible Rule #11:
People can get a bit funny if you use the F-word.
No, not that F-word. I mean *feminist*.

My day does not actually improve.

I mean, a meeting with the Head and your parents is bad enough, but now add in Dad looking a bit stoned and refusing to take off his sunglasses and Mum wearing a low-cut top (she thought it might make Mr. Ambrose treat me more leniently). Even Mum's boobs couldn't save me. I had to write a letter of apology to Zara or I'd get kicked out of school. Also, I have to get the clip taken down. I'm actually not too bothered by the clip at all. But a letter? Normally, I would come up with a cunning plan to get out of this, but lack of breakfast stopped my brain from working. So who's the rebel now? Letter written and handed over. That really, really hurt.

By the time I get home, my head is spinning and my stomach is so empty it's rumbling like a volcano. All I've had is an apple and Diet Coke all day and it's starting to show. Not where I want it to, around my tummy, bum and legs, but in my temper, energy and eyes. And this is only Day One.

I think about what to cook tonight. I could just waltz in and say, "I'm not cooking tonight," but then we'd all starve. Dad's too lazy; Gran, Mum and Cat seem to be in a competition to see who eats the least; and Lauren is too small to take care of herself. I love the joy of cooking and the joy of seeing people eat my food. But I'm not feeling any of that today. I'm beginning to realize why Cat is in such a foul mood pretty much all of the time. Because being hungry all the time absolutely sucks.

So tonight, my heart's not in it. I bake white fish with ratatouille. There's some bread for those who want it. I add what flavor I can with garlic and fresh basil, plenty of salt. Salt may not be great for the heart but it's got hardly any calories and it tastes great. How many things can you say that about?

About six thirty they all start to troop in.

The kitchen is full of rich tomato smells. Hey, I've gone a bit wild and thrown some white wine in with the fish. Only a few calories and it's worth it for the flavor.

"Family meal night," Dad says like some made-for-TV version of himself. "I've been looking forward to this all week. After today, we deserve a little treat? I know it's not Thai curry but it smells good." Dad loves Thai food — I think he spent a long time in Thailand taking "recreational" substances. He is his mother's son, after all.

I serve it up. Five plates of fish in wine and lemon, and Mediterranean vegetables. No oil. No carbs. Just light protein and veggies.

Dad looks down at his plate and I think I'm about to see a grown man cry.

Lauren says, "That looks disgusting. Alice says it looks disgusting. She doesn't like vegetables and I don't like fish." She pushes the dish away with disgust. "When's pudding?"

I say nothing and begin to eat. True, it's blander than I would normally make. You can only do so much with tomatoes.

Dad says quietly, "Is there any sauce?"

I shake my head. He nods and begins to eat without any enthusiasm.

Mum and Cat eat quietly without comment. I think that I just miss a flash of eye contact between them. I refuse to look at them.

If I was on *MasterChef*, what would Nick and the fat one say? "The vegetables are soft, pleasant in texture and full of flavor. The fish is well seasoned and light. However, the whole thing lacks substance and creativity. It is not the worst meal that I have ever eaten in my life. But it's far from the best."

But it is food. And I'm hungry, so it is gone far too quickly and I still want more at the end.

I finish first. Lauren and Alice are arguing about which exactly is the most disgusting vegetable on their plate. Dad looks sad. Mum and Cat are eating in the same way that drives me mad — small bite, chew twenty times, swallow, drink water, repeat.

Mum starts, "This is very pleasant ..."

"Thanks," I reply.

"It's a bit different from your usual," she says. "What's the inspiration behind it?" I look to see if she's laughing at me, cos if she is, I will take a kebab skewer and plant it right between her eyes.

"Summer," I lie. "The weather's getting warmer and I thought a light meal would be nice."

Mum nods and says nothing.

Cat doesn't have such tact. "Are you trying to lose weight?" she asks.

Part of me is reeling cos Cat has actually said something. Part of me is reeling cos Cat has hit on the truth.

"You think I should be?" I reply.

She shrugs. "I'm just asking."

"Do you like it?" I ask. "That should be the only reason to eat food."

She tuts at this and stops eating.

"Are you full?" I say.

"I've had enough," she replies.

"That's not what I asked," I push.

She stands up and walks out of the room.

Mum glances at me. She pauses. "Jess. Firstly, I'd like to thank you for cooking such a lovely meal. But you could be more sensitive. You know it's a difficult subject for her."

It's just food — where did it get so complicated?

There is silence.

Then Dad asks, "What's for pudding?"

I look him in the eye. "Fresh fruit and fresh air." I listen hard; I think I hear his heart break. And probably mine, too.

After dinner, I go to my room to do some homework. I mean, if I'm going to be allowed to sit my exams, then I suppose I should do some work. At least it keeps me occupied.

My phone pings. I look at the screen. It's MATT.

Hey, got into any fights today?

Heart pounding, I reply.

Nope, not yet. But will start practicing mud wrestling later.

LOL — sounds fun. Send me a photo if you do. ;-)

But then I'm distracted as Lauren comes in, all sobbing, and gets into my bed.

I wonder what Alice has done to her now.

"What's up, shrimp?" I ask her. "This is not a good time."

I quickly type out, Sure. Am in my Lycra suit already. A bit saucy but look at me flirt.

"I don't want to get married." Lauren sobs into my pillow.

"Why are you thinking about marriage?" I ask her. My phone is silent. He's not responding. What did I say?

"It's the end of *The Little Mermaid.*" She shudders and sits up. "Ariel gets married and goes off and leaves her daddy behind. I don't want to leave home, I don't want to leave you, I want to stay here forever."

With that, she hiccups and cries big, snotty tears. I hug her and try to avoid the snot. I stroke her hair. "Lauren, you can stay here forever. No one has to get married unless they want to. You don't have to get married."

I keep looking at my phone but the display remains dark. I stroke Lauren's hair but my mind is on messages. And Matt. Maybe he's just busy. And he was the first to text, after all.

Lauren seems to calm down a bit at this. And then falls asleep in my bed. I look at her in wonder. I wish I could be four. No rampaging hormones that make you behave like a cave woman when you're really aiming for a more sophisticated look. Four-year-olds don't worry about what they look like or if boys like them. Or spend half an hour pondering every possible meaning that a text message could have. My phone is as responsive as a stone.

I think about where I can go where there's no food. Gran.

So, I carry Lauren, snoring, back to her bed and I go up and see Gran. She's watching *The Maltese Falcon*. Sam Spade is cool and the women are awesome, all attitude. I do like films like this. If I had a waist, I'd put on some super-slim jacket, paint my nails and lips red, start to smoke and get myself into some ungodly mess.

"Ah, Jesobel, my love," Gran murmurs when she sees me. I lean over and kiss her papery soft cheek. "Get your old granny a top-up. Only a half, mind." And she winks.

"Top half or bottom half?" I ask with a smile. This is Gran's favorite joke when pouring a drink.

"Always the top!" she says. I pour her a generous portion of whiskey and pop in three ice cubes from the freezer compartment of her little fridge. She nods approvingly. I look at her profile. She doesn't seem that much like Dad. I've seen pictures of Granddad. He died before I was born and he didn't look much like Dad either.

I sit at Gran's feet and lean against her. She strokes my hair. I feel like crying.

I tell her about Lauren and *The Little Mermaid*.

Gran snorts. "You should tell her the real story, the one where he marries someone else and it's torture, every step she takes. Now that's a story to cry about. Too highly strung, that child. Full of nonsense." She takes a sip. "But then maybe she instinctively knows that marriage is a way to repress women. She might have a point after all."

"She's only four," I remind her.

"When I was four, I got a hard smack on the bottom for silliness and, frankly, that child is silly at times. She lives in a fantasy world!" Gran knocks back the contents of her glass and asks for more.

"What's it like being married?" I ask to distract her.

She looks at me with a steely glare. "Why, are you thinking of giving it a go?" she says. "Patriarchal nonsense. Why should a woman change her name and just become a piece of property to a man?" She pauses, still searching my face. "But why are you asking?"

This makes me smile. Then something happens that makes me smile even more. My phone buzzes and it's Matt's beautiful name that shines. Did someone say Lycra?

"No plans to get married," I lie. I mean, a girl likes to daydream. "I've just been thinking." What can I send back? My fingers tap away while Gran talks on. Sorry. You missed it. What a pity. Maybe you should dig out yours in the name of equal opportunities??

"Both thinking and feeling are overrated in my book," Gran says crisply, oblivious to what I'm up to. "Best to just get on and make the most of things."

"Is that comment related to marriage?" I continue.

Gran pauses. "Perhaps." She sighs. "I loved your granddad, but he was hard work. Marriage is tiresome. It just wears you out after a while. We only got married because I got pregnant, and it made our tax situation easier. So even I've conformed from time to time."

She turns to Humphrey Bogart. He's quizzing the bad guy. Life looks more glamorous and less complicated in black and white. I wonder if Bogart would text back straight away or would he keep a girl waiting?

"The whiskey helps," she says.

"You do know I'm too young to drink, and that you drink too much?" I say. My phone goes. Sounds fair. Wait ... Did you hear that?

"Pish, I was at parties every week when I was your age. Started going to protests then, too. Got a bit tipsy from time to time. It wasn't the drink that was bad for me, it was the marriage."

What should I have heard? I know I should be giving Gran my full attention as she's giving me all this insight into her life, but I'm currently squirming with joy.

Her eyes go bright for a moment and I feel terrible for texting when I should be listening. "I don't know what they mean by drinking too much. I'm an old lady with few pleasures. And two of them are in the room at the moment." She strokes my hair again. That almost feels as good as seeing Matt's name on my phone.

"There's so much I don't know about your life, Gran," I say.

"You can't even guess." She smiles. "But I'll tell you one secret if you like."

"Go on," I say. She nods toward her bureau. "Third drawer down," she says, holding out a small key with her ancient hands.

I carefully take the key from her, unlock the drawer and pull it open. I take out an old photo, all curled and yellow round the edges. A cool-looking brunette with clever eyes smiles out from it. She's wearing denim and her arm is around a younger version of Gran. This almost distracts me from my dead phone.

"That's the only person I ever really loved," she says.

"But ..." I splutter. "But ..."

"Yes, I know she's a woman. But that's where my heart led me. For a time."

She smiles at my open mouth.

"So, your silly old gran isn't quite what you thought. You have no idea, really, my darling, about what my life's been like. One day we need to have a proper talk. For now, pour me another drink and get yourself one while you're at it."

My phone comes to life again and so do I. Did you hear that sound? That was my mankini ripping when I put it on.

"Jesobel, are you ill? You're suddenly gone all flushed. You're not shocked, are you?" Gran peers at me with concern.

"Not shocked, just surprised." I think Gran would be shocked if I told her I was bright red due to the rather glorious mental image of Matt in hardly any clothes, so I keep that to myself and pour her another drink. My hand trembles as I pour. The thought of Matt in ripped, flimsy Lycra is making me tremble all over. Does he think like that when I text him?

Despite all Gran's wise words about relationships, one thought grabs hold of me.

I wonder what sort of wedding dress would suit me?

CHAPTER THIRTEEN

Invisible Rule #13:
Never tell the truth. I mean, really, don't.
No one ever really wants to hear it.
Just tell yourself the truth.

After a restless night where I kept waking up with all kinds of hot thoughts boiling round my brain, I try to think of something that will cool me down. School. Yup, that will do it. What's my first lesson? PE. Yup, that will pretty much kill off any flirty thoughts that I might be having.

And before I know it, there I am. Getting ready for Physical Education. You might think that as a larger person, I might hate PE, but I do like to confound and confuse if I can.

See, normally PE can be fun. Stay with me. Cos it's fun to see how serious some people can be about an activity that is essentially moving a ball around. Let's think about that for a moment — sport is usually about moving a spherical object from one location to the next while making it as complicated as possible. This is true for football, rugby, netball, cricket and golf, to name but a few. It's similar with track and field. How can we move from one place to the next as quickly as possible, often placing irrelevant obstacles in the way to make it harder? Some call this challenging yourself. I call it stupid.

I find PE amusing for these reasons and because this is when all the various elements of the school come together in a context that involves direct rather than indirect competition. The sporty, the fashion conscious, the swots and the geeks — all present, and all worlds collide. Often literally.

But currently, I'm not thinking about that. All I can think about are my texts. I've read through the exchange so many times I know it off by heart. If only there was an exam in memorizing messages from attractive guys.

All of this means that I'm just sitting in my gray uniform thinking colorful thoughts when I should be getting changed. "Come on, Jess. Stop dawdling," Hannah nags as she puts on her sports top over her school shirt. We all do this and then shuffle out of our uniforms without ever revealing bras or more than an inch or two of flesh. It strikes me as it never really has before that this is all very silly. I mean — look at them all! If the worst crime a girl can commit is to be fat, then I'm the only one who should be sent to jail. Why should anyone else hide away? Tara is tall and leggy like a model. Hannah is all curves and hair. Izzie has the most amazing ankles. You can't diet and get ankles like that — you have to be born with them. The futility of the whole eating-less thing gets to me. Or maybe I've just not been eating and lack of breakfast is stopping me from thinking rationally?

Lara — I think, but to be honest it could be any of them — takes issue with even my quick glance. "Jess, stop looking. Are you a pervert as well as a freak?"

I have broken the first rule of the girls' changing room, which is never look at each other's bodies. Lara won't shut up. "Tilly, she was looking at my boobs."

Okay, she's not playing nice so I don't see why I should.

Deep breath, Jess, and attack. "I have no interest in your boobs. In fact, now you've mentioned them, I'm struggling to locate them. Do you in fact have any at all?" What makes the difference between my friends and Zara's is that Hannah and Izzie just maintain a respectful silence rather than take part in a group attack.

Lara's face begins to crumple, but I'm tired of being made to feel less when I am more. So I find myself unbuttoning my shirt. "Now I may be fat. But these are boobs." I jiggle the aforementioned body parts for full effect. I might be going too far but it's strangely liberating. Lara is edging away. "Good idea, Lara. I mean, if I turn around too quickly with these girls, I could quite possibly knock you out. These are my boobs of mass destruction." At this point, Lara just squeals and runs away.

"Jess," says Hannah with a tone of strained patience, "can you put your boobs away and behave like a normal person. What the hell is going on?" That is a very good question. In my defense, I do think lack of food is beginning to affect my judgment, so I do as I'm told and put on my sports kit. Mass destruction averted.

"Come on, ladies, let's get lively!" Our PE teacher bounces up and down like a hyperactive terrier. "Jess, at least I won't have to send you to the Head today for uniform infringement." She looks at my regulation PE skirt and laughs. I don't crack a smile. Though part of my brain — the bit that's still capable of thought — does process this. Two days ago, my short skirt = rebellion and chaos. Now my short skirt = uniform. Context is everything.

While she witters on about rules and technique, I think about calories. I was going to have a run this morning but, what with the sleep deprivation, that went out the window. This is a good opportunity to burn some fat.

And then we're off. Thirty girls, some of whom really don't like each other, are armed with lethal pieces of wood and let loose. There's a TV series to be made here. Put us in more skimpy outfits and we'd be TV gold. Sporty Amy plays as if every kitten in the world will be impaled upon spikes unless she gives it her all. But she's not alone today. As I count up how many calories I could burn, I suddenly find myself running around like a crazy person, too. Because I am.

Forty minutes later, I am feeling wobbly. My stomach hurts, my brain's numb and my hands are shaking. This is only Day Two. How will I ever make the next three weeks and one day? I tell myself that these feelings are good. That it's working. I am supposed to be hungry.

"Are you okay?" Hannah says, as I prop myself up on the hockey stick.

"Yes. Just might be going down with a bug," I say. I'm getting bored of this same old lie.

I don't think that she quite believes me but she's too good a friend to disagree. I stagger off the field and get changed.

The rest of the day is a blur. Then form room at lunchtime. Normally, I would be tucking in to my home-prepared lunch. No mass-produced crap pretending to be healthy for me. Only now I'm not eating anything.

Hannah looks closely at me. "Where's your lunch?"

I have put some thought into how to answer this question. I need to be vaguely plausible. "With all the stress this morning, I forgot. I'll pick up something later."

Izzie looks so shocked that she stops reapplying her mascara for a second.

I give her the stare. "I refuse to eat anything that this school makes. It's a matter of principle. Anyway," I say with a shrug, "I'm hardly going to waste away."

Then an animated expression takes hold of her. She stares at me. "You do look odd, you know. And you've not really been eating much. OMG. She's doing some weird spell on you."

"What are you talking about?" I say.

"Zara, of course. She hates you, we all know that. Maybe she's hired someone to put a curse on you. I mean, you not eating is just not normal. You have to admit that."

I'm about to say, *No, I* am *eating — just not very much*, but then this would be admitting that I'm not eating. Me. Who has mocked every single girl in this school who has ever said this.

I can explain this, or I can let Izzie continue with this madness that I am affected by an evil spirit. To be honest, it's all a bit much.

And that's when I black out.

What happens next? Well …

1. I come around, they take me to the nurse, she asks me lots of questions, I tell lots of lies. Dad comes to pick me up. He looks worried, but not worried enough to stop winking at the nurse and signing an autograph for her. Turns out, she's a fan of his best-known song.

2. We go home. I don't eat dinner.

3. I go to bed but I can't sleep cos I'm hungry, so I eat a small green salad and some fruit.

4. I get up for school the next day. I don't eat much.

5. My head hurts, my stomach hurts, I feel like I want to die.

6. Zara puts a copy of my apology letter on her Instagram feed. Matt likes it. My heart breaks a bit when he does that. Alex doesn't and calls her out for being snide.

7. The dress hangs in the corner of my room. It smiles at me. I don't smile back. But I still don't eat.

8. Hannah takes down the clip. But not before the blogger behind *Fat Girl with Attitude* gets in touch. Yes, Imogen, my fave-ever blogger, wants to do an interview with me. I've got her personal email. She's just a few taps of the keyboard away. But I don't reply. Why? Well, the girl in the video clip is not me at the moment. Not sure when normal service will be resumed. It's just three weeks now. I can do this.

9. But can I?

At school, I just go through the motions. Gossip wafts around me. Head down, I just take notes in class and try to make sure that I have everything I need to review.

At lunch, I refuse to go to the dining hall. "I've got something yummy left over from last night," I lie. "I'll eat it in the form room." I tell so many lies now. I'm exhausted just thinking about them.

Izzie puts one hand on my left shoulder, Hannah puts another on my right. "Okay, this is crisis time. Form room, now!" And I'm marched back there to be joined by Sana, Suzie and Bex. Once there, Bex puts the chairs into a circle and I find myself sitting down facing a ring of friendly but concerned faces.

"Circle time?" I ask. "Like when we were five?"

Hannah snorts. "Shut it, Jess. Now, we, your friends, are worried about you." I try to interrupt but she keeps on going. "Firstly, you do not appear to be eating. The Jess we know and love always says that eating is her biggest pleasure. Secondly, you blacked out in PE. Thirdly, a blogger who you admire wants to talk to you. But you won't. As you will see, we have a range of opinions on what the matter is."

"You would make a good lawyer, you know," I point out. She ignores me in a way that makes my point.

"Izzie thinks that you have been cursed. Bex thinks that you are subject to alien influence. Suzie thinks that you are having a meltdown." Hannah pauses for dramatic effect. "I, however, having reviewed all the evidence, have come to a different decision. I think that you, Jesobel Jones, are trying to lose weight for reasons unknown."

Busted.

So much for all my lies.

I feel tears pricking in my eyes. These are my friends who just want the best for me. And I'm lying to them because I feel stupid about what I'm doing. Generally, I'm the strong one, the one who goes her own way, the one who doesn't care about what other people think. And yet here I am counting calories like the girls I've always laughed at. I've never felt so weak.

"Of course not," I start, but my voice betrays me and begins to wobble. "Maybe ..." Now my voice disappears completely. I put my head in my hands and the tears really start now. God, what an idiot!

But if I am an idiot, at least I'm not on my own. I feel but don't see the hugs of Hannah and Izzie while Sana and Bex say soothing things. It takes a few minutes but slowly I begin to calm down until I can manage to speak. "Bex, alien influence? Really?"

She looks ashamed. "It seemed more plausible than you just stopping eating for no reason."

Izzie says, "But are you sure that you've not been cursed? Have you experienced any strange phenomena when Mrs. Brown is near?"

I look her in the eye. "I can promise you, hand on heart, that I'm not cursed."

She looks disappointed. "Shame, I have a really cool counter-curse that I was dying to use."

"Have you been binge-watching *Buffy* again?" I fire back. Now she's the one who's busted.

"This is all well and fine," Hannah says, "but it doesn't clear up one thing. Why are you doing this?"

I can't answer. Whatever respect they've ever had for me will be gone.

"I just ..." My words run dry again.

Somehow, Hannah knows. "Is it the party?"

I nod.

"Oh."

Bex looks at me with a slight squint. "You're trying to lose weight for that Matt boy's party?"

I nod again. "I know. Pathetic."

Izzie says, "No, Jess, not pathetic. Just normal. That's what lots of girls would do."

"But I don't want to be normal," I start to howl. "I want to be different."

Sana pats me on the knee. "And that's why we like you. But it's also very reassuring to know that even you have off days."

"What do you mean?"

"You can be a bit intimidating sometimes, you know. Always waving cakes in people's faces when they say that they're watching what they eat." It's true. I do do that. Just think of those cupcakes a few days ago. "It's nice to know that even you can feel insecure at times."

"All the time. I just try to fight it."

Izzie smiles her big daft smile. "You don't need to fight all the time. It's too exhausting. But there are other ways of fighting back. Just by sticking together. That's what friends do, right?"

Now that's the most magical thing that I think she's ever said or done.

CHAPTER FOURTEEN

Observation #6:
It gets tiring being judged all the time.

I'm still thinking about that on the walk home. But at the moment, the walk seems beyond me. I have to walk about twenty minutes. Downhill. It's not exactly like climbing Mount Everest or even rolling down Mount Everest, which I imagine is quite hard, what with all those rocky bits and the odd hungry yeti to deal with. But even walking down this hill seems like a marathon when you're hungry. I've gone beyond actually feeling any hunger to just having a constant slight headache and a general sense of being Rather Unwell. I wonder if I lie down and roll, I could get home without any level of effort at all. Okay, it might look a bit crazy. I can imagine all Mum's friends. "Is Jesobel all right? We've just seen her lying down in a road and rolling down a busy street. Thank goodness I'd just put down my almond decaf soy latte and was watching the road, or I'd have squashed her head like a watermelon." Watermelon would be good — very refreshing and very low in calories. Is food all I think of? Er, yes, because I'm practically STARVING MYSELF.

It is at this moment that I realize I am in a perilous situation. I am in desperate need of food and I am standing next to our nearest convenience store. It sells chocolate. It sells chips. It sells all manner of delicious, though processed, food that might give me enough energy to get home. Internal dilemma begins: Old Jess says, "You've eaten nothing all day. You fainted yesterday. This is not healthy." New Jess whispers, "You'll never look good on your wedding day to Matt unless you starve."

I don't know what to do. I mean, I'm not really intending to get married until I'm in my twenties anyway, and that's a very long time to go without eating. Maybe I'll find one small snack with a teeny, tiny number of calories. There might be a miniscule pack of nuts, not salted, of course, because that would be too much like taste. Nuts are good for you, aren't they? No one's looking so …

"I hope you're not going to get a snack."

I jump back as the beautiful, gaunt specter of Cat looms in the doorway. I'm not sure how someone so thin can loom. Maybe it's more that she lurks. Anyway, in short, Cat is standing in the doorway, staring at me with laser eyes as if I'm about to eat a bagel. With lots of cheese. The double sin of carbs and full-fat dairy. I start to mumble, "I was going to …" but my voice trails away. I don't even have the energy to lie to my sister properly. What is wrong with me? (Rhetorical question — I NEED TO EAT!)

But my brain does work enough to ask one question. "What are you doing in there?" Surely, Cat doesn't have food in secret. Does she nibble like a rabbit on a huge block of dark chocolate or shove salted caramel popcorn down her throat in handfuls?

"I came for this, of course." She waves a bottle of water in my face. "Still, I find sparkling water makes me bloat." She taps her flat belly as if to make a point.

"Fascinating," I reply. Ninety-nine percent of me wants to make a sarcastic reply about how bubbles of gas can't make you fat, but I'm too tired and also it strikes me that this is the second conversation I've had with Cat in three days. Which is huge. So, I don't want to blow it. Instead, I find myself wandering after her. "Farewell, unsalted nuts, our time will come another day," I whisper back to the shop.

"Are you talking to yourself?" Cat spins round.

"Only to the shop. It's the only sensible conversation I get some days," I fire back.

We walk in silence for a few paces. So back to normal, then. Cat surges ahead, as if we're in a race. Am I supposed to keep up with her or trail behind like a needy child?

"Do you have to walk so fast?" I blurt out.

"Don't you want to burn off fat? This is the perfect fat-burning pace," Cat says, as she taps the fitness tracker on her wrist to measure her progress. "Yes, heart rate at optimum level."

I stare at her in awe. This is the longest conversation we've had in weeks, and I'm seeing her in a whole new light. My heart is full of Matt, but hers seems to function just as a workout tool. I'm not sure which of us is right, but she's off down the road, long legs pumping at such a rate that I have to almost run to catch up with her.

"So …" she says as I puff alongside her, "what are you planning on cooking tonight?"

"Did you like what I cooked the other night?"

"It was better than your normal carnival of fat and salt."

"I like to think of it as worshipping at the temple of flavor." I'm thinking "carnival of fat" my arse, but then my arse is wobbling as we walk, and Cat's tiny bum just propels her legs forward without so much as a jiggle. Like Mum, she is a jiggle- and giggle-free zone.

Cat gives me a side glance. "But you have to admit your choices aren't healthy."

This is getting personal. "Many vegetables and innocent salad items are slaughtered during the preparation of my meals, so I refute wholeheartedly any suggestion of lack of vitamins."

"But you use fat, cream, butter, cheese." She spits the words out as if just saying them will make her blow up to the next size.

Breathing heavily now, we sweep past our house. Are we going on a walk? Where is she taking me — a quick stroll round all of the UK? But if I want to keep talking to Cat, I need to stay with her, so I just fire back, "These are all elements of the well-known Mediterranean diet that contribute to long life and good health."

"We've been to France. It's full of fat old women who get their flabby boobs out on the beach. I'd rather die than turn into that, so you can keep your Mediterranean elements, thank you." Cat strides majestically on.

"Well, I was thinking of chicken in a Thai glaze on a green salad," I shout after her.

She pauses for a second. "Sounds good." She stops and turns to look at me. "Jess, are you trying to lose weight?" When she asked me this before, I lied. Do I still lie? Why does it even matter?

"Maybe," I find myself saying. "Just a bit," I hedge. "I mean, I'm not made for skinny." Cat walks around me now, eyes scanning up and down, measuring me with her precise gaze. It's worse than standing in my underwear.

"Hmm," she says.

"What?" I say.

"Nothing." She keeps walking. "I'm just thinking."

"You're clearly thinking about me and this is all entering the territory of Very Weird." I peek round. "You are staring at my arse, Cat. In public." She keeps staring. I give her a good shove. "Stop it. Tell me what you're thinking."

"You're not going to like it," she warns me.

"Well, I'm not exactly loving it at the moment. Spit it out."

Sighing, Cat begins. "You've got a lot of work ahead of you. I mean, we're talking years of willful overeating here, so you're not going to put that right overnight."

"But I've less than three weeks," I whisper.

"What?" Cat leans in to hear what I'm saying.

"Er, nothing, I'm just inwardly sobbing."

"Good, you need to. You're reasonably in proportion apart from being top-heavy, and nothing but surgery is going to sort that out."

Really? Surgery?

"You do have a waist of sorts, but obviously, it's far too big. Don't leave the house without plenty of Lycra on underneath, for starts. Wrists and ankles suggest that there might be hope for you once you get rid of all the blubber."

I like to think that I'm quite tough. I mean, I've survived the best that Zara and her crew have thrown at me for years. But my sister talking about my blubber makes me think a) I'm the subject of that Great American Novel that no one ever actually reads or b) I'm about to be harpooned and brought to shore. I turn away so she can't see my eyes brimming with tears.

"Jess, didn't you hear what I said? There's hope."

I sniff and find some words. "Hope, yes, that's great."

She peers closely at me. "You don't look that great."

Will she never give up? "I know," I say, "you've made that very clear."

"That's not what I mean." Then she says the one thing that I would not have expected. I'm feeling a bit faint anyway, but this nearly has me falling to the pavement. "I think you need something to eat."

CHAPTER
FIFTEEN

Observation #45:
Guys work out to get bigger.
Girls work out to be smaller. Go figure.

With that, she's off again with me trailing after her like a weak puppy. Fortunately, we're home soon so my poor legs can finally buckle. Cat is in the kitchen and beginning to chop things like a girl possessed.

"Okay, Jess, you really don't have the hang of cutting back on eating. You've made a rookie error. You've gone right to starvation mode, and your body can't take it." She's slicing something green like it has personally offended her.

"Oh, I think I can take a few days of eating less, thank you very much."

She turns to me, knife in hand. "I don't think so."

"Can you put that down, Cat? You're starting to scare me. Are you making me a snack?"

She sniffs but at least she lowers the knife. I was beginning to think Jess kebabs were on the menu tonight (but, then again, I don't think Cat would eat anything with such a high fat content).

"You look like you need a smoothie."

Hallelujah. My taste buds are singing. I can almost feel the sugar starting to rush through me, bringing me back to life. "Can you put mango in?" I start to gibber. "Or banana. I love bananas. If we had some raspberries, that would be perfect, but I think I used them all yesterday. I find that if you add a touch of icing sugar and lime …"

"Jess. Stop." She's got that dangerous look in her eye again. "No mangoes. No bananas. No raspberries."

What madness is this? "Then what kind of smoothie are you making?" I stare in horror at what she's getting from the fridge. "Everything's green."

"Like I said, rookie errors. You can eat. Only a fool would not eat. But you need to think very carefully about everything you put in your mouth." She steps in. "Like now, Jess. Step away from the nuts."

I look down. My hand has crept out and found the bowl of almonds that Mum leaves on the table to encourage healthy snacking. I'm just about to eat one. I didn't even know I was doing it. "Just one nut, Cat. It's not even got salt on it."

She slaps my hand down. "Are you serious about this or not?"

I think of the dress. I think of Matt looking on adoringly as I walk toward him, how the sun bounces off the tiny gold highlights in his hair. I think about how close his face was to mine only yesterday and how badly I wanted him to kiss me. I think of Zara's face if she saw us together.

"I am serious." I make a big deal of putting the nut in the bin. "See, I've passed the test." I'm not prepared to tell Cat the whole truth yet, but I'll give her enough to put her off the scent. "So, Mum bought me this dress but it's a bit tight. I just want to fit into it."

Cat seems to accept this.

"So, tell me again, what's going into this smoothie and will I like it?"

"Firstly, it's a kale, broccoli, cucumber and coconut water smoothie. Secondly, it's irrelevant whether you like it. It just needs to give you energy."

This is not okay. "Food should be enjoyed." This seems to annoy her, as she's now chopping the kale into tiny pieces. "Is that fun?" I ask. "Or does cutting them this fine make them less calorific?"

I get a raised eyebrow but at least that's better than a glare. "Very funny. I just like to do things properly."

"Why don't I chop and you get the blender out?"

Cat thinks over my proposition. "Can I trust you? I mean without constant supervision, you were about to eat a nut."

"I was. I'm a bad person." I make what I hope is a suitably sorrowful face. I channel what Lauren does when she's caught out eating chocolate for breakfast. "I've learned my lesson and will not try to sneak in anything that's not green."

"Okay, you chop and I'll get the broccoli." Ha, now who's made a rookie error? I grab a very ripe, very delicious avocado. While Cat is rummaging through the salad drawer, I split it open and cover the flesh with kale leaves. Which is a bit tricky as Cat has cut them so small.

Thing is, she's so light, I don't hear her creep up behind me. "I don't think so." I spin round and she's right behind me, flourishing a head of broccoli like it's a weapon. "And you promised."

"I didn't lie. Avocados are green. And very good for you. Even Mum eats them. Every celebrity who Instagrams their breakfast eats avocados." I wiggle one in her face. "It's only little." I grab a pen and draw a face on it. "Look at his little cute face. It's Anthony the Avocado. Don't make him cry."

There is a hint of a smile. "You are ridiculous, you know."

I shrug. "It's the lack of food."

Cat puts all the veg in the blender. "You really want Anthony to go in? I mean, you say you don't want to upset him, but you're the one who wants to blend him." She dangles a bit of avocado over the blades and then lifts it to her ear as if listening to it. "What's that, Anthony? You're too young to die?"

I stare at her. "Cat. You're talking to an avocado. Have you gone mad?"

"Like you say, lack of food can do that to a girl."

"I have a thought. How about we save Anthony and add just a drizzle of manuka honey. Even a date or two? That's natural sugar, right? No harm there." Now, I know there is very little nutritional difference between a date and a spoon of sugar, but it's amazing the number of people who don't. Will she fall for it?

"Okay. A very small drizzle of honey."

Hurray — flavor wins. I mean, this smoothie may still be an abomination but at least it stands a chance now. Before Cat can change her mind, I grab the honey from the cupboard and put a dollop in the green gloop that she has created. After mixing, I pour it into two glasses, handing one to her.

"Bottoms up." I clink glasses with her. "Here's to all the poor green things that have been slaughtered just for us."

"Cheers." Cat clinks back. She takes a sip. I take a sip. She makes a face. I spit my sip back out into the glass.

"Hey," she protests. "I made that for you. It's full of nutrients."

"I am eternally grateful. I will try it again, but you have to look me in the eye and say that you're really enjoying it."

She purses her lips.

"Go on. Look me straight in the eye and say that this is the most delicious smoothie you've ever had."

She can't even look at me.

"I'll drink it all. I swear I will. Every last semi-blended broccoli floret. But you have to say you love it."

Cat's mouth is beginning to twitch.

I won't give up. "Come on, you can do this."

She takes a small sip, then looks at me. "This is the most —" Then she breaks. "Oh, I give in. It's hideous." Then she starts to laugh. "It's like drinking compost."

"Compost that a cat has weed on." Then we both explode.

At this point, Dad shuffles in looking bemused. I don't think he's seen his daughters laughing together for some time. "Are you okay?" he asks.

Despite the fact that I'm still starving, I manage to reply, "Yes, Dad. We're fine. Never better. Now, I'm going to whip up something light and delicious for Cat and me, and I can make you an espresso at the same time if you like."

"Sounds good." He slumps down, humming to himself. Cat sends me a small smile. And that is really rather tickety-boo.

CHAPTER
SIXTEEN

Invisible Rule #49.7:
All women must worship shoes. But more than thirty minutes
in heels and my feet start to bleed. #lovesneakers

Which is not how I'm feeling a few days later. Hannah and Izzie have been poking and prodding me for hours now to make me look acceptable for my maybe date with Matt. I look in the mirror. What looks back at me is best described as half girl, half pony. I'm all huge hair, braids, smoky eyes and ripped jeans. I asked them to make me into a rock chick, but I feel less like a rock chick than a total idiot. Even Mum is in on this. Izzie has somehow persuaded her to let me borrow a pair of £500 shoes. The good thing about this is they apparently make my legs look longer. The one drawback is that I can't walk in them. No one else seems to think that this is a problem.

"What time is it?" I ask. Matt's coming at seven thirty, or so his last text said. I had been watching the clock manically all day, but the whole makeover thing has distracted me.

"Nearly time for your carriage to come and pick you up," Hannah quips. Matt has a car, which is another thing that makes him utterly wonderful. I've never been alone with a boy in a car before. Tonight is just going to be one first after another.

Izzie's looking worried, and given my general level of anxiety, I start to panic. "What's up? Do I look really awful? Do I look fat?"

Now Izzie just looks horrified. "You have never uttered that phrase before in your life. Where is our Jess and can we have her back?"

"She's lost under all this hair spray, currently choking, but normal service should soon be resumed."

The doorbell goes. We all look at each other and do a little scream. "Okay, time for a quick selfie." We huddle, pose, the flash goes off and I hurtle to the door.

"What are you doing? Put this on your Instagram! Beats all those food pictures you keep posting," Hannah says as I rush past.

Izzie cautions, "Be cool, Jess. We'll tidy up and then let ourselves out."

"Thanks," I say. I'm off, heart pounding.

But the sight that greets me at the bottom of the stairs doesn't do anything to calm my nerves.

Standing right next to the huge photo of Mum as a stunning young model is the aforementioned mother herself. Except that she looks very much like she's flirting with *my* date. He looks like he's just wandered off the front of some magazine, all gelled hair and white smile. She's giggling, she's flicking her hair. She is in general behaving like a four-teen-year-old. Normally, I would stomp down the stairs to annoy her, but I don't think that stomping would make me look hot, so I try to copy Cat's gazelle-like grace. Trouble is, I've not done this before, and after a few steps, I lose my balance and slip down the rest on my bum.

Annoying Mother–1, Jess–0.

"Hey, Jess." Two words. He's looking down at me because I am lying at his feet.

"Hey," I return. This is not what I had in mind. I stand up, beyond embarrassed. "I see you've met my mum."

"Yeah," Matt replies. "You're coming along later?" he asks her.

Mum shakes her head. "I've spent years of my life watching Stephen play. I'd rather stay in. But you two enjoy yourselves." She looks at the shoes that I'm carrying. I wince and offer them back to her in the hope that she'll take them off me.

"Izzie said it would be okay but if you'd rather not, I'll wear something else."

"Despite Izzie's goth tendencies, she does have good taste. She's picked out a good look for you. You could learn a lot from her." Thanks, Mum, for basically calling me unfashionable in front of Matt. "So, keep the shoes. But if you damage them, they cost £500 to replace." With that, she drifts off. "Enjoy. I want to hear all about it in the morning. But back by eleven, Jess, it's still a school night."

"I'll get you home by then," Matt says. He looks at the shoes. "Wow."

"I think I'll wear trainers," I find myself saying.

"No." He looks up at me and grins. "No, these are things of beauty and you've got to wear them."

"Really?"

"Really!" We "reallied." It's our thing.

Something like joy floods through me. He opens the door and waits for me.

"Right, I'm coming. I'm really good at walking in general so don't be alarmed by any sudden lurches. You've seen my natural balance in action already." I teeter across the floor, my balance of gravity leaning forward with my toes being squashed into the tight points of the shoes. "I have absolutely got this."

"If you say so." Matt smiles. "Though you might be pleased to know the car is just outside. So, you don't have to walk, or should I say wobble, far?"

"This is not wobbling," I fire back. "All the women in France walk like this. It's very refined. Très chic in fact."

"It's certainly something." Is he laughing at me or with me? He clicks the key fob and the lights flash on his black Mini. I really want to take a photo of this just to show Izzie and Hannah later but that wouldn't be cool. There is also another problem.

"Give me a moment."

"Jess, are you coming or not?"

"I'm in the process of moving. I'm just taking a break."

"Is walking to the car too hard for you? Do you want me to drive up onto the pavement?" he teases.

"No, I'll be okay in a moment." I pull and pull up at my foot and I'm still not moving.

He looks at me with a patronizing smile. "Heels stuck in the pavement?"

I step out of them and yank them free. "That's better. You may call them things of beauty but I call them ridiculous." As I climb into the car, I recognize what he's playing. "Great choice."

"To get us in the mood," Matt says as he pulls out. I start to hum along to one of Dad's later records, now blasting out of the stereo.

In the mood for what? That's what I desperately want to know. But with the music so loud, there's no chance to talk. He's commented on the shoes but not the new hair or look. Does that mean something or nothing? I may be stranded in Friend Zone, but the whole evening is in front of us, so I try to keep my nerves under control while I think up good topics of conversation. It's not far to the venue where Dad's playing, an old cinema that's now a trendy bar with the auditorium area set up for big parties or small gigs. In the day, it can look a bit tatty, but tonight, in the May evening, it seems bathed in light and possibility.

"Looks jammed," Matt says as he taps his long, tanned fingers on the wheel. I try not to feel jealous of an inanimate object and force myself to pay attention to what's going on.

"Pull over here and we'll walk that last bit."

He looks at me quizzically. "Given that you're rather challenged in the walking department, maybe we should try and get nearer. Or I could carry you."

Now, at some point in the last week or so, I may have daydreamed about being carried in some sort of way by Matt. Perhaps on a walk after falling in the sea. Perhaps he tried to pull me up and then I pulled him back into the surf. All those things may or may not have been dreamt about, along with a few other dreams that I'm keeping strictly in the mental file of VERY VERY PRIVATE. But in all those dreams, I looked smaller. The thought of him carrying me now — or even joking about it — is currently labeled WORST NIGHTMARE EVER.

"I am a twenty-first-century girl. I can walk in heels, just watch me. Pull over, driver." I wave my hand regally at him and Matt parks up.

I'm not so regal when I can't get out of the car, as it's so low. But somehow, I manage to smile, giggle and get myself into a standing position. On my second attempt at walking in these heels, I note that I've made huge progress. I do move forward and I only get stuck in the cracks between the paving slabs twice. Just when I'm internally cursing the shoes and swearing only ever to wear flats and trainers again, I wobble and find that Matt has grabbed my arm to keep me upright.

His hand with those gorgeous fingers is now touching me. Okay, Dad's leather jacket is between us, but still. This is more exciting than the moment my double-cooked cheese soufflé rose and stayed puffed. Oh yes, even better than that. And certainly less calorific. We exchange a smile, and we walk toward the venue, arm in arm. Cars are beeping outside and there's a scrum of people all ready to get in. The bright flash tells me that the press are here. I'm going to a secret gig and I'm turning up literally on the arm of the most beautiful boy I've ever seen.

There might not be a red carpet but there's a corded-off section with security on it, while everyone else is waiting on one side. "Jesobel Jones plus one," I say, with more confidence than I feel, to the very thin woman wearing huge sunglasses who's managing the queue.

"Jesobel, did you say?"

"Yes, Jesobel Jones as in the daughter of Stephen Jones. You know, with the band?"

A pause.

"There you are. Jesobel plus one." She lifts the rope and we walk through. Lights pulse in our faces. "Names," yells the photographer. I can't see him, as my eyes are still dazzled by the light.

Matt says, "Jesobel Jones, daughter of Steve Jones, with Matt Paige, groupie."

And with that, we walk in. Together. There's photographic proof.

This is now officially the best night of my life.

CHAPTER SEVENTEEN

Invisible Rule #35.5:
Guys have got to make the first move. Poor guys — just
imagine the stress. Another great reason to be a girl.

See, I love high heels. Haven't I always said that high heels are the most amazing invention EVER? Yes, you can't walk in them and you keep falling over. But surely that's a small price to pay if it means a gorgeous guy takes your arm. I can hear Gran's voice yelling at me, *You're making yourself a victim to attract a man? Jesobel Jones, I brought you up better than that.* But I shut her out because I don't want thoughts like that to burst my perfect bubble of happiness.

The hall is packed with a range of people: Dad's old rocker friends, perfectly groomed women of a certain age and a random selection of ultra-hip millennials. I'm probably the youngest person here. As I peer at the crowd, looking for faces I know, I get uncomfortable. No one's dressed quite like me. No, I needed sunglasses, a bright red dress and Vans. That's the look most of the women sport here.

Matt grabs my arm tighter. "Don't look, but Joss McFarlane is over there."

"Uncle Joss?" I reply. "The little guy in the very high boots? He's really got a thing about being five foot three inches. I'll introduce you if you like." Inside, I'm doing a little happy dance.

Matt gapes at me. "Uncle Joss?"

"I mean, he's not my uncle, but I've known him since I was a kid. I think the story goes that he drank from the font at my christening. Apparently, he was thirsty after a big night out," I say, feeling that tingle of joy all over again. "Come on." I take a step, wobbling like Bambi after a few too many vodkas, and walk with as much determination and grace as I can.

"Hi, Uncle Joss." His leathery face breaks into a huge smile. He might be a legendary singer to some, but in our house, he's the bloke who Dad hangs out with to tell his own version of war stories. All Matt can see is me talking to a legend.

"Jess! You've grown. Look at you, girl." I get a hug.

"This is my friend, Matt."

They shake hands. "Great to meet you, kid."

"I'm a big fan. I really love your work."

Uncle Joss waves him away. "So, Jess, you're here to see your old man. He'll be made up by that." I nod, but then others come, surround him and bear him off. He turns to wave. "I'll see you later, Jess. Looking good, kid."

Matt stares, his mouth still hanging open. "Problem?" I ask.

"No, just a bit overwhelmed."

I whisper, "Welcome to my world," but Matt doesn't hear over all the background noise.

"I can't believe I've just spoken to Joss McFarlane. The man's a legend."

"A legend you can find in The Dog and Partridge every Friday afternoon. Drop by and buy him a drink. He'll tell you stories that will blow you away."

"I'm seeing you in a whole new light. You really are full of surprises."

"Oh, you've seen nothing yet," I say with confidence.

The air is humming with music, perfume, drink and expectation. "Have we got time for a drink before it starts?" I suggest.

Matt nods and leads me by the elbow to the bar.

"Hey!" Matt gives the guy next to him a huge bear hug. "I didn't know you were coming or I'd have given you a lift." He slaps him on the back and then steps back. It's Alex.

He grins at Matt and nods at me. "Hi, Jess. You look great. I think I see touches of my sister's work."

I blaze a warning look at him. He mustn't give the game away about how much effort went into getting ready. I want Matt to think I just happen to look like this without any effort. I don't want him to think I need a team of girls to make me look presentable. "Don't know what you're on about." Alex looks bemused and is about to speak when the house lights dim for a moment.

"Let's go," says Matt. Suddenly, we're caught up in the crush to fight for a place at the front of the stage. People are pushing together to get a good view; I'm shoved into Matt, who puts his arms around me to make sure I don't fall. Thank goodness it goes dark so no one can see how much I'm blushing. I'm surprised that nobody is shouting, "Call an ambulance — that girl's on fire." But they don't, because four figures shuffle on stage in the blackness and then the first few chords ring out.

It's a strange experience seeing your father on stage. At home, we regard him as a kind of cute but useless pet. You love having him around but he serves no point whatsoever. And watching him play, I feel so bad about this. It's like he's shed a skin and become someone else. He struts, his hands fly up and down the strings, he inhabits the stage. There's so much noise I don't think anyone hears me shout, "Go, Dad," probably the most uncool words ever uttered at a gig. As for what they're playing, it's a cover version of an old classic but no one cares — all anyone wants to see is the four of them back together. I can see how Dad's looking at the crowd, feeling the love and growing visibly taller every second. In a moment, he'll burst through the roof. You and me, Dad, I think, we're both on top of the world. I flick a look up at Matt to see if he's feeling the great vibes, too. It's not Dad he's looking at, but the singer. And he's not just singing along, he's copying his stance, staring as if he's absorbing every move. Matt returns my gaze. "This is awesome." And it is.

The next hour or so flashes past. After a few cover versions, they fall silent and then one long guitar note hangs and hangs in the air. And then it's like thunder. They launch into the old hits — a wall of sound hits us and the energy is ferocious. It might be four fifty-year-olds on the stage but they sound intense.

"Just like the old days," someone shouts next to me.

"Better than the old days — they've lived it, they've earned it." Great reply, I think. I'll never look at Dad the same way again. He *has* earned this.

By now, we're moshing, leaping up and down, bodies crashing into each other, terrifying and exhilarating at the same time. I'm going to topple over and crash. I can feel myself going. But Matt grabs me back just as the music comes to a huge roaring climax. The crowd goes wild, the guys walk off and then the lights come back up again. I hug Matt without even knowing what I'm doing. Then I tense — what if he doesn't hug me back? What if he just pushes me away?

But he doesn't. Those arms just hold me tight, and for a moment, every cliché comes true. I'm lost in my own world of joy. Bombs could drop around us and I wouldn't care. He's holding me, he's looking at me and I'm looking back. The only thing that could make this moment any better would be if he kissed me. His lips are inches from mine. I can feel his breath on them and he smells delicious. There's a faint smile on those lips and he bends toward me.

It's finally going to happen.

All kinds of crazy begin to explode inside me.

But then disaster strikes.

CHAPTER
EIGHTEEN

Observation #89:
If men had periods, more time would be spent
researching painkillers. Just sayin'.

My ankle wobbles, the shoe goes and I go with it. Instead of locking lips with Matt, I'm sitting on my fat arse on the rather sticky floor, being looked down on — in every sense — by all the cool people. This was not the way I planned it. Matt reaches down and hoists me back up again. Being hoisted is the least romantic thing that can happen to someone.

"You okay?"

I put my best brave face on. "Yes, but now I know why they are called killer heels. I'll be back in a minute." I need time out, and that drink from earlier means a trip to the toilets is in order. Off I career, walking from pillar to pillar, still struggling to do the very simple task of moving from one place to another. Would Mum kill me if I broke the heels of these things? I mean, I'm her daughter. What woman would choose a pair of shoes over her daughter? I shake my head, stupid question. Mum once said she'd sell us all for a fully funded shopping trip to Paris and I don't think she was joking.

The second I'm behind the door, I rip off the shoes and squeal with delight. My toes are singing with joy but secretly sobbing at the same time. They're all red and crushed together, and a nail has cut into another toe so that the inside of the shoe looks like a Halloween massacre. And all this for beauty?

"Great shoes but they're a bugger to wear." I look up to see a girl a few years older than me, large but rocking a sparkling blue catsuit, redoing her fabulous makeup in the mirror. I take note of how confident she looks. She's not draping her curves in baggy shirts and layers, like I do.

"I love what you're wearing," I find myself saying. "Where did you get it from?" As she tells me the name of the online shop, I decide that she looks familiar. Is she looking at me the same way? It's all a bit awkward. "Sorry to stare, but I think I recognize you from somewhere," I say.

With eyes narrowed, she's still assessing me, and then a broad beam of recognition crosses her face. "You're Fat Girl!" I wince. Oh yes, on so many levels, I am. "Sorry, that came out wrong. I'm Imogen Hattersley. I blog a bit. I didn't mean to be rude, but you're from the clip, aren't you? 'Fat Girl vs. Mean Girl?'"

Then it hits me. I'm talking to Fat Girl with Attitude. "That's me," I say. "Half, well, maybe two-thirds, of the clip is standing before you."

"Cool," she says, "I love that video. I played it when I was feeling down. Before it got taken down, that is."

I look at her, bemused. "You don't."

Smiling as she expertly applies her lip gloss, she says, "Yeah, you know, when I have a fat day ..."

"A fat day?"

"A day when you feel fat and don't like it. A day when someone says something nasty about how you look or you can't fit in your favorite jeans. Well, when I was having a fat day, I watched that and how cool you were, and then it made me feel that I could take on the mean girls, too."

Wow to infinity and beyond.

There's too much to handle here. First, I'm cool. Second, I'm an inspiration. I feel like asking, *But don't you just see how big my belly is?* But I don't, because a) I don't want to spoil the moment and b) it's clear that she didn't notice at all.

"That's the first time someone I don't know has recognized me," I say. "I think this is my fifteen seconds of fame."

"Isn't it fifteen minutes?"

"I think since the Internet came along, the whole world got a lot faster."

She laughs. "Well, the Internet has a lot to answer for. Cute cat videos are great but it's a Wild West for people like us."

"That's so true. But you have a really great blog. I love reading it."

"We are the fabulous fat people of the North West!"

I start to babble. "Your posts are great. You say what I think and feel, only better. And you look fabulous! I struggle with fashion." I gesture down at my clothes. "My friends helped me out tonight. But I love your pictures. I need to start shopping where you do."

She holds out her hand. "So, I'm Imogen. What's your name, Fat Girl?"

"Jesobel but everyone calls me Jess."

"You should totally go with Jesobel. Jesobel is a name with attitude. Well, Jesobel, if you want to, I'll take you shopping sometime."

I know that you shouldn't arrange to meet people you only know from the Internet. I know that there is a small chance that she's some crazed stalker who will kidnap me, kill me and then impersonate me by wearing my skin. But I don't think it's very likely. The strange thing is that I feel like I know her already.

"I would love that." I look at myself in the mirror. "I don't know what my look is. I don't think this is my look. I feel like I'm at a fancy-dress party."

"It's hard," Imogen sympathizes. "I think you look great but no look is going to work unless you like it."

My false eyelashes are starting to droop and fall, and the sweaty heat of the room is doing nothing for my lashings of mascara. "Here." Imogen takes one look at my sad face and starts to fix me up. For someone who can cook, get good grades and generally cope at life quite well, I seem to spend a lot of my time being fixed up by other people.

"Now, that's better." And it is. We get out our phones and swap numbers. "I'd love to stay but I have to be off. How strange to meet you here! I have a thing for nineties' one-hit wonders. What brings you here?"

I feel a sense of pride for Dad, though I don't think that has ever happened before today. "I'm Steve Jones's daughter."

Imogen claps her hands in glee. "Perfect. Of course you are." She looks thoughtful. "Okay, Jess, I think it would be really cool if you wrote something for my blog. I emailed you, didn't I? But you never got in contact."

Oh my days.

"I'd love to …" I start with a rush of emotion. "But I'm just not sure what I'd have to say that would be of any interest."

"Nonsense. I've got to run. I need to write this up for a newspaper and get it out before anyone else does. But I'll be in touch. Good to meet you, Jesobel Jones." And with a hug, she's off.

I look in the mirror. Imogen wants to go shopping with me. Imogen is my new best friend. I'm so excited by this, I've completely forgotten about Matt. Or about going to the toilet. Getting those jeans up and down is an ordeal, especially with the long fake nails that Hannah has stuck on me, and it takes ages. The nails are a HUGE issue when … let's say, you could easily remove/damage important parts of your anatomy if you're not careful with them.

All hot and bothered, I rush as quickly as the shoes will allow. They really *are* just a patriarchal instrument to stop women taking an active part in life. I peer through the crowd for Matt, but spot my dad instead. He's surrounded by friends and fans, but I wave enthusiastically and give him a big thumbs-up when he sees me.

That's all good — my daughterly duty is done. But where is Matt?

I see a tall figure leaning against one of the pillars in shadow. "Matt?"

He steps forward. I sigh with disappointment. "Hey, Alex. Do you know where Matt is?"

"I do. Can you walk in those shoes?"

Vaguely annoyed by him changing the subject, I say, "Evidently. I was there. Now I'm here. I think you just saw me walk. Why?"

Alex seems amused. "Nothing. It's not your normal look, that's all."

"A girl can have more than one look. A girl can express herself through clothes however she wants."

"Of course a girl can. I just thought that you would normally laugh at shoes like that and say that they are a patriarchal way to oppress women."

I look at him in surprise. Is he a mind reader? Instead, I just sniff. "I don't take fashion advice from a Ron Weasley wannabe." It's a bit cruel but he just laughs. "Seriously, where's Matt?"

A shadow passes over his face. "He sent me to wait for you. He's sorry but an amazing thing happened. He got talking to a promoter who's interested in the band, and they've gone off to listen to the demo we did."

"Oh," I say. The word *oh* can contain so much. Like, *that's great for him but what about me?* The best night of my life has peaked too early.

"I'll give you a lift home if you like," Alex offers. I had really been looking forward to the lift home. All warm and cozy in the Mini. Matt's hand on the gear stick, inches from mine. I might have accidently brushed it while getting something from my bag. The chance of a goodnight kiss. All gone. Oh.

"That would be great." I look around. Dad's busy, Matt's gone, even Imogen's just disappeared. There's nothing here for me.

I take the shoes off. "I've decided I don't like this look anymore."

Alex grabs Mum's heels from me. "I accept that you can express yourself however you wish but these are stupid shoes."

"I never want to see them again." I sigh. With one expert throw, he chucks them in a nearby bin.

"Alex! They cost £500!"

"Waste of money. You could get a good guitar for that."

I scrabble through the bin. "You idiot, I've got to give them back." Thank God, they're just on the top so I don't have to get my hands too far down in the rubbish. "It's not funny."

Alex thinks otherwise. "It's a bit funny. And you think they should be there, really."

"Maybe. I think they're great. Unless you have to walk." I'm suddenly very tired. All the days of anticipation, all the hours to get ready, all the emotions this evening. And here I am, removing a pair of shoes that I don't even like from a bin.

"Can you take me home?"

"It would be my pleasure."

Going home on my own is not how I imagined this night to end, I think sadly. But then I remember the party. I do have a second, final chance.

CHAPTER NINETEEN

Invisible Rule #61:
Only thin people can exercise. Which is
ridiculous whichever way you look at it.

To fill the void of not eating, and to distract myself from seeing if Matt texts at all, I play some poker with Gran. She says it keeps her mind sharp, and she beats me every time, so there's nothing wrong with her mind. But normally she takes keen enjoyment from beating me, and this time her mind doesn't seem to be with us.

I'm waiting for her to have her turn and she's just staring into space. "Gran?"

She slowly moves her focus from wherever she was. "Ah, yes," she mutters and promptly drops her cards. This is not the Gran I know and love. As I bend down to collect them all up, I notice that she's drifted off. My phone rings and she doesn't react. Normally, she makes some sarcastic comment about how my phone is permanently attached to my hand and that I'm a willing slave to technology, but this time ... nothing. It's Hannah, and I want to take the call but I feel a little guilty.

"I'll be back in a bit," I say. Mental note to self: I need to do something here. But first — Hannah.

It's hard to know what she's saying as she's squealing like she just found a first edition of *Sense and Sensibility* in the charity shop for 50p. When I finally start to get some sense out of her, Hannah is babbling about a website that I have to go on. Phone in hand, I find the site she's going on about.

I'm at it again. For someone who has no interest in being famous for anything apart from beautiful macarons, I do seem to keep finding myself online.

On my screen under the headline "Chip Off the Old Rock," there's a huge photo of me and Matt taken from the other night. It's a blog about Manchester news and it's full of shots from the gig. Including this one. As Hannah continues to communicate in a high-pitched tone that is only audible to dolphins, I ignore her and focus on the photo. It is, I have to say, a glorious shot. In black and white, just to be extra moody, it's overexposed so that our faces are super white and every angle is emphasized. Matt's cheekbones are to die for and me … well, I look okay. The mega hair and panda eyes don't look ridiculous. They look … I look … good. It's like someone's taken my daydream of me and Matt hanging out in permanent bliss and turned it into reality. I'm almost winning at life again. Matt and me in public, close together, like a couple, for all the world to see.

By this time, Hannah's voice has almost dropped to a normal level and I can hear what she's saying. "Zara will explode when she sees this." I agree and quickly copy the photo to my Instagram feed. Take that, Zara.

My stomach rumbles and I try to ignore the ache from the constant hunger that's always with me. It gets me down, but moments like this make me think that it might be worth it.

Hannah's tinny voice has spoken while I was distracted. She repeats herself again. "Well, what are you going to do next?"

"You mean, how I am going to get on the Internet again?"

"Don't be silly. How are you going to get closer to Matt? You have his number, don't you?"

I do, but I don't like using it unless I have a purpose. "Well, Alex said that I should go and watch the band rehearse, so maybe I'll do that."

Hannah goes silent for a moment. "Wait, do you think that's a very bad idea?" I ask.

"No, I'm just wondering if we can use Alex at all. He's gone a bit moody on me is all. He gets grumpy and stalks out if I ask him anything about Matt, so I don't think he's going to be any help. But, yeah, that sounds like your next move."

I've been planning it for days. But the thought of texting him makes me sick to my stomach. He might say no. Even worse, he might not reply. Being in limbo is better than being rejected, so it's easier to do nothing. I also think lack of food might be at the heart of my inaction. Currently, just lying on my bed all evening seems to take up all my energy. Oh, yes, and then Cat drags me out for some workout from hell. But Hannah and I chat on for a bit and I promise that I will text Alex to make sure that it's still okay to go, and then I can tell Matt that I'm going. I tap out a quick text to Alex, and shortly it's decided that I'll go to the next rehearsal in two days. That bit is easy. Then my fingers hover over my phone. What do I say to Matt? I can't stop looking at the photo of the two of us. It would be a stretch to say that it's a photo of two people who are madly in love. We're looking at the camera and not at each other. But his arm is draped around me. We look like we fit together. And that's the first time I've felt that.

If I want anything to happen with Matt, I can drift around hoping that fate will just draw us together. Or I can do something. So, I text him.

Nothing.

Even more nothing.

My phone buzzes; my heart races as I grab it up.

Not Matt but Izzie. Have you seen Zara's feed?

Why do I get the feeling that I don't want to see it? I scroll through pictures of perfect smiling girls and perfect food to find Zara's account. It's a bit of a strange one for Zara, whose account is normally nothing but highly filtered pictures of her wearing very small clothes and pouting like a fish.

It's an image of a pig wearing lipstick.

I don't get it. But then it hits me. That old saying — a pig that wears lipstick is still just a pig. That is, you can't change someone's true nature. My stomach lurches like I'm in a lift, dropping. She means me. I'm the pig.

Zara–1, Jess–0.

*

In the morning, I feel a bit better until I remember about not eating and that I have a physics test in a few hours. But the one shiny thing that glimmers on the horizon is the rehearsal tomorrow night. That keeps me going through a long thirty-six hours of near starvation and manic exercising with my sister.

Hannah won't go with me as she's got a thing about the band. She thinks Alex is a better singer than Matt and, though she doesn't say so, clearly thinks Alex should be the lead. Izzie says loud music hurts her aura so she doesn't want to go. That means that yours truly ends up standing outside a church hall on her own, feeling like the original Billy No-Mates. I think Izzie might have made the right decision cos currently my ears are feeling somewhat stressed and I'm standing outside in the graveyard. I think even the long-since-departed are probably hearing this. I'm not even sure I want to go in because a) I'm nervous and b) I don't want to end up having to lie if they are absolutely terrible. The second option is even more terrifying when I consider that they are supposed to be playing at our Leavers' Ball in a few weeks.

"Coming in or not?" Alex is suddenly standing beside me.

I jump like I've just had an electric shock. "Don't do that! I thought I was alone. Aren't you supposed to be inside?"

"I'm late." I follow him in as he opens the huge wooden door for me.

Suddenly, the vibe changes. It goes from full-on thrash metal (I do hope that's not what they play for Leavers') to just a guy and a guitar.

Matt sits on the edge of the stage, his fingers picking out a melody on the strings. He's in his own little world but there's something magnetic about him. I know I'm obsessed with him but he just looks like he's in the right place. He's barely doing anything but it's just so EXCITING!

Then he starts to sing. It's a bit croaky to start off with, even I will admit, but his voice has real power and a gorgeous rocky rasp that makes him sound like he smokes and gargles with whiskey. It's an acoustic version but soon his voice is bouncing off every rafter in the building.

"He's good," I whisper to Alex.

"Yep, he's certainly got it."

"What?" I say, not able to look away from Matt.

"Star quality. There are better singers out there but he just looks …"

"Like he belongs there," I finish.

Alex nods ruefully. I wonder about his sad face. An old memory surfaces through. About two years ago, I'd gone on holiday with Hannah and her family to their holiday home in Wales. We'd spent an evening on the beach, under the stars with the waves crashing in the dark, while Alex played his guitar next to a fire. Goosebumps suddenly appear on my arm and I shiver. Alex notices.

"You're cold? Do you want my jacket?"

"No, I'm fine. I just remembered how good you are at singing. Remember that night on the beach in Wales?"

"You remember?"

"'Course. Well, I'd forgotten but it's just come back." I look at Matt and then at Alex. "You know, I'm not sure who I would say is the better singer."

Alex laughs. "That's the thing. It's not just about the voice. It's also about the looks."

Awkward. Clearly I fancy Matt but I don't want to be a cow. "You sing if you want. You're great. It's about the confidence, isn't it, not the looks? I think Mick Jagger is hideous but I like watching him perform."

"So, you're saying I'm hideous?"

The smile suggests he's teasing me, but still, I end up backtracking. "Of course not, I'm saying great singers in bands are about the voice and the stand. If you stand as if you're rooted to the stage, like it's your place, then that's what matters. You can do that if you want to. It's all in the head."

A burst of applause breaks out. I stop looking at Alex and realize that Matt is standing there; the set is over. He's looking at me and Alex with a raised eyebrow. Immediately, I stand up and start to applaud enthusiastically to make up for my momentary distraction. Matt leaps down from the stage and is up with us in a few strides. As I admire how he does it, I can't help but think that if I did that, I'd fall on my face somehow or break the floorboards when I jumped down, turning myself into a re-creation of Rumpelstiltskin.

"Hey, Jess. How's things?"

"Great," I say. "Fantastic set."

He glows in my praise. "Glad you liked it. You should bring your dad down one night."

"He'd just end up on stage with you and try to steal the limelight."

Matt leans in. "But that would be awesome. Alex, persuade her. Get her to bring Steve down."

Drily, Alex says, "I'll leave the persuasion to you. But Jess was just telling me what a good singer I am."

Confusion clouds Matt's lovely face. "You were talking about Alex during *my* set?"

Alex might be smirking but I could kill him right now. The only heavy object on hand is a large bible, and that would be wrong on so many levels, so I just kick him. "I suddenly remembered hearing him sing, that's all. But we *both* agreed that you look like you belong on stage."

Have I saved the moment? This is not going as planned at all.

"Okay," Matt says, "but who is the best singer between the two of us? Who's better — me or Alex?"

Ouch. Matt looks at me; Alex looks at me. I look at the floor. Come on, Jess. This is your moment. Forget about Alex, it's Matt you want to impress.

"On tonight's performance, you edge it."

Alex's face falls; Matt starts dancing around. "Burned, man. Ha, I'm the best." Then he stops. "What do you mean, I edge it? That I'm only a bit better than him?"

"I chose you. Enough," I say. Time to change the subject. "Did you see that article about the gig that had a photo of us on it?"

"Show me," Matt says and so I get up my feed.

"Sweet," he says and takes his phone out. "Gotta put this out there." As he does so, he drops it. Not just me who's butterfingers, then. I pick it up and the photos are open. I can't resist having a quick scroll through but then I see something that I really wish I hadn't.

I hand the phone back, suddenly sick to my core. "See you later."

Matt grabs my arm. "Don't go. You've only just got here. Alex, tell her."

"Stay for a bit. You should hear us all play."

And so, I stay. But my heart's not in it. All I can think of is what I saw and what I'm going to say to Cat.

CHAPTER
TWENTY

Invisible Rule #15:
If a boy sleeps with a girl, he's cool.
If a girl sleeps with a boy, she's a slut.

Going to the rehearsal was supposed to be all about me and Matt. But like a gone-off strawberry in an otherwise perfect cheesecake, what I saw on Matt's phone spoiled the whole beautiful time for me. Maybe I got it wrong. I just don't think I did and now I don't know what to do. I can't concentrate at school. All I can think about is what I saw.

As I picked up the phone, there was a photo of Matt, and Jack, and Jack's ex. Jack and the ex weren't kissing but they were hanging all over each other. I can't even say it was an old photo because one thing I do know about Jack is his obsession with the latest fashion. That was a new shirt. He wore it to our house last week. There is no way on earth the photo is more than a few weeks old. So, at some point in the not too distant past, he was hanging out, up close and personal, with his ex. When he was supposed to be going out with Cat.

Now what do I do? Telling Cat is the logical option. But the problem with bad news is that people tend to shoot the messenger. I'm the messenger and Cat would probably pin me to the floor with some weights, leaving me in the basement to starve until I was a skeleton. And even if I did tell her, what would I say? I've no proof. It was just a photo on Matt's phone.

I could ask Matt about it. But something makes me hang back. We're not proper friends, so asking about it might seem weird. Then I have a brainwave.

I'll ask Alex.

He's one of the good guys who would hate the idea of a guy cheating on a girl.

He'll tell me the truth.

I get myself out of eating lunch by saying I need to make a call. Sana purses her lips in disapproval, but it's only a few more days till I can get back to worshipping at the altar of food. I find a quiet spot somewhere and text Alex, quizzing him on what he knows.

He gets back to me straight away. That's one of the things I like about him — everything seems so easy with him. No waiting for hours for him to get back to you.

Beyond that, he's not much help at this point. Yes, Jack and his ex go to the same parties sometimes. But that doesn't mean anything.

I interrogate him via text. No kissing?

None.

Holding hands?

Pause. Perhaps once or twice. But it is just holding hands.

Wrong answer. Holding hands is for best friends or people you fancy.

I stand corrected, great leader.

Alex promises that he'll tell me if he sees or hears anything definitive. I'm back where I was — full of suspicions but knowing nothing for sure. Is it just because I really don't like Jack?

Cat and I train for a bit after school. I try to make out what's going on inside her head as she pushes herself harder and harder. If I was in a relationship, I would want to know everything that my boyfriend got up to. It feels awful to know something and not say it.

But I stick to our family tradition and say nothing. Just like we don't talk about what's going on with Gran. I lose myself in the next few days, in studying, exercising and dreaming of the food that I will eat once that fateful party finally comes.

And then, it's here.

Three and a half weeks since the invitation. Three and a half weeks of feeling rubbish. But finally, the day I've been waiting for dawns. My second and only chance I know of to get Matt to *really* notice and like me.

I don't know how much weight I've lost, if any, but I figure that today I can eat. Whatever has or hasn't happened to my body, today won't make any difference.

I open our fridge. Dad pretends to be environmentally friendly but that didn't stop him and Mum buying the biggest badass fridge known to humankind. Even Americans might find our fridge excessive. I keep opening it and expecting some penguins to come wandering out. Fortunately, all I find are the ingredients for scrambled eggs, smoked salmon and bagels. Yes, bagels. Pure white carbs. Food for fat people.

I put on some coffee, blast some Beyoncé, split the bagels, crack out the slightly salted butter and begin to make the best scrambled eggs this side of the Pennines. A dash of cream, a shaving of cheese, these babies are gonna be fab!

I pile it all high, first the bagel, with a slab of butter, then the salmon, as much as I can bear, then the hot, salty, slightly cheesy eggs. I breathe in deeply for a moment and then begin to eat.

The heat, flavor and salt explode in my mouth. The butter starts to melt and the glorious burst of salt and fat makes my body sing. For a few minutes, my mouth is in ecstasy and my stomach slowly begins to sing hallelujahs as it starts to realize that normal service has been resumed. I'm not sure that I feel happy, but I am starting to feel full. I am the girl who eats life again. In fact, it's like I've been lit up with light bulbs from the inside — every nerve seems on fire.

Dad comes in and looks at my plate. "Looks good, kid," he says.

"It is," I say, "I made it."

"Any left for your old dad?"

"I can make some more," I say. "But you'll have to wait."

He goes to the iPod and searches through. His iPod is full of Oasis, Blur, all the guys who were doing the business when he was. His finger stops scanning. He finds his song. He looks at me; I smile.

"I like it, Dad — it's one of my faves. So, put it on and turn it up."

Dad blasts it out and smiles at me while I make him the best brunch I can manage.

"You're a better guitarist than Noel Gallagher," I say.

He smiles. "God hates a liar." But he glows just like he did on stage. I keep finding him reading reviews of the gig and laughing to himself.

My phone goes. I let Hannah and Izzie know what time to come over and confirm that, hell yes, I am ready to party. This is not true. Parties are generally considered fun events, and yet my stomach is currently deciding whether to enjoy the hearty and delicious breakfast that I have lovingly made or reject it and see it slide all over the granite worktops.

I did have strange dreams about Matt all night (well, most nights). One was particularly bizarre, where we were about to be shipwrecked and then a large shark ate him. I could look on a dream website to find out what that was all about, or I could just trust my instinct. The shark did have a look of Zara about it. All teeth and dead eyes.

I go upstairs. The day stretches out before me and I have no idea what to do. So, I cyberstalk Matt again. The photo of me and him framed in the camera flash comes up. If only I can make that beautiful moment happen again. I need a plan. Do I shower now? And then again later? This is not the night to be in any doubt about my level of cleanliness. You don't want to be having an intimate moment and then it all goes horribly wrong cos the guy's gagging over your sweat problem.

Izzie's arrived, complete with candles, incense and hair straighteners. Bless her little heart. We're getting ready here rather than the basement cos there's more room and easier access to a bathroom. As this process could take hours, we need space and comfort!

Then Hannah arrives and we look at the mound of stuff on my bed. Checklist:

1. Makeup tutorials online, showing us all we need to know about looking like a hot girl

2. All the makeup that we either own or have secretly borrowed from our mums

3. Clothes that will transform us from ordinary girls into goddesses that boys will want to snog and then our lives will be complete. Hmmm.

Izzie says, "I'd like to do a ceremony before we start."

Hannah and I look at each other.

"Now, before you two roll your eyes, I want you to remember that we are all friends and, as such, we should respect each other's ideas. If you don't like what I'm about to propose, then just think of it as either positive energy or, worst-case scenario, an opportunity to laugh at me. All I'll say is — remember Rebecca Turner."

We do. We remember that Izzie thinks that she arranged that unlikely union. A union as unlikely as me and Matt Paige.

"I'm in," I say, my normal doubts pushed to one side.

"Me, too," Hannah follows. "What do we do?"

Izzie should be a film director! She shuts the curtains, lights a ring of red candles and then Hannah and I sit at two points of a triangle. Izzie makes the final point and throws red petals in the middle as she hums some weird tune.

"Take a candle," she then commands.

We do.

"Repeat after me," she says.

We do.

> "Spirits wild and spirits free
> Look on us, a willing three.
> In our hearts lies secret love
> Grant our wishes from above."

I'm not sure if the spirits are poetry critics, but if they are, then I think they might find this a bit rubbish.

"In your third eye, see the face of the one you love. Visualize it as intensely as you can."

I think of Matt looking up at me that first night I saw him, how his long hair fell into his dark eyes, the smile that played round the corners of his lips and his eyes. How, for a second, I felt a complete connection with him and how I've replayed this moment over and over again. I hold on to this, as if wishing will somehow bring him into the room.

On the count of three, we blow out our candles. We sit in the gloom for a minute. We wait. Izzie gets up and opens the curtains. "That should do it," she says.

I remind them, "We've got a party to go to and we've got to look great."

CHAPTER TWENTY-ONE

Invisible Rule #29:
A girl can't just turn up to a party.

I'm sent for a shower while Izzie and Hannah scour the mags for ideas. Then comes the tricky business of getting rid of pretty much all your body hair. Cos while the hair on your head is supposed to be long and glossy, God help you if there's any other hair ANYWHERE else! Any dark hairs on limbs or under limbs or in unmentionable places must be removed. Two options: a) close encounter with a razor (danger — stubble alert!) or b) wax. Waxing is made to look so easy in adverts but last time I tried, I stuck myself to the duvet.

So, in these circumstances, a girl's best friend is Veet. It's pink, it smells funny and it dissolves your hair. Not particularly natural, but then neither are hair-free legs. I'm wearing skinny jeans, so I'm not quite sure why I think my legs should be hair free, but you don't suddenly want to find yourself in a position where hair-free legs might be a good idea and then shout out, "Hang on a minute, keep that thought, I'm just going to the bathroom, and excuse the industrial smell when I get back."

I'm doing it now. Just in case.

I smear thick pink gloop over my legs up to and including my bikini line. Then I smear it all over my armpits. Not much going on there, but I may as well do a proper job. Now I have to wait five minutes. Only I've forgotten to put the timer on and now I've got to set it with slippy pink fingers. I wonder if the gloop will dissolve my phone, so I wipe the stuff off my fingers onto the towel (Mum will love me) and then try to wipe it off my phone without canceling the timer. This is not a good start.

I'm sitting naked in my bathroom, perched on the edge of the loo, covered in pink gloop, waiting for the timer ring.

I hope this is not a symbol of my life to come.

There is little dignity in this moment but it's the end result that I'm hoping for.

I play a few songs on my phone and check out the buzz on the party tonight.

I jump when the harp rings out to tell me that it's time. I take my little scrapey bit of plastic and scrape as if my life depends on it. A few rebellious hairs refuse to go. I'll get them on Phase Two with the razor.

I shower at length. My skin feels great, thanks to the super-strength conditioner they put into the gloop. No hair on legs or under arms. I clearly went a bit mad on the bikini line, as now I seem to have nearly given myself a homemade Hollywood. I've turned myself into a porn star! I can hardly stick it back on, so I'm left with a small triangle of hair.

Okay, all bad hair gone. Now, the good hair! This gets washed three times, followed by two conditioning treatments.

I think I'm done. I put on my PJs and dressing gown. Hair first, then makeup.

"Right," I say, "this time I want to look like this." I show a picture of the makeup I want. "No rock chick this time. I want to look more vintage glamour."

Hannah peers at it. I wait for her disapproval but she just says, "That would work for you." I glow. I can do this — look great but look like me. Izzie does a nice job with my hair. My once wavy locks are poker straight and shiny. In another twenty minutes, Hannah's hair is a set of stunning red curls. Izzie even manages to transform her fake black hair into glossy dark curls that any Hollywood star would be proud of.

We look in the mirror together. Result — three girls who look like girls in a magazine. Hannah and Izzie giggle. I gasp.

At first, I think it's a mistake. It doesn't look like me in the mirror. My eyes are normally a bit small and pudgy. Now they look huge, and they blaze brightly. My whole face looks different. Big eyes, big lips, big hair.

I peer closely and then back away. The reflection does exactly what I do. This girl in the mirror clearly is me, but it's a better version. An airbrushed, perfect, plastic me. Better than the rock chick look, for sure. I wish I could look like this all the time. Can you add a filter to your appearance so you can always walk about looking your best?

Hannah, Izzie and I look at each other and we smile. We all look great — no one needs to boost anyone's ego and no one looks better than the others. We are all as hot as we'll ever be.

Our makeover has delivered its first goal. We are a step further away from being ourselves. But does that bring us anywhere nearer to what we want?

The final part — getting dressed. At this point, I feel sick to my stomach. Yes, I look pretty. But then no one has ever really said that I'm ugly. So, that's not the issue. The issue has always been the F-word. Maybe the bagel was a bad idea after all.

I stare at the wardrobe. I can almost hear the dress laughing at me, teasing me for dreaming that I could wear it and not look ridiculous.

I've not dared try it on yet and I don't want to put it on in front of them. If all my fat is still hanging out, it'll be too much to bear, even in front of my best friends.

As if Hannah senses my anxiety, she says, "I just want to call Suzie about a few things. I'll be back in a minute." Then Izzie decides to go to the toilet. It's just me and the dress.

Who cares about winning some kind of competition with an inanimate object? Apparently, I do. Mum has thoughtfully bought me a pair of Spanx. I believe Adele swears by them. So, that's okay. Why go on a diet when you can just damage your internal organs by encasing them in gut-busting elastic?

I open the wardrobe. The dress glows in the dark, its blue softness alluring. It's not quite what I'd normally wear and the danger is that it's not quite the same as what everyone else will wear, but over black skinny jeans, it looks like something out of *Vogue*. I don't have a backup, there's no Plan B. If it doesn't fit, I don't know what I'll do.

I take a deep breath. I put on my jeans and zip them up. Then I pull the dress over my head. It slips down. For a moment, I can't bear to look at myself in the mirror.

And then I do.

I feel like crying.

It fits. It looks good.

I'm not thin but I'm thinner. I almost look like what Mum would think is normal. I look more like Mum; I could look like Cat. I might not be top of anyone's snog list but I wouldn't be an embarrassment. I stare at myself in disbelief.

There's a knock at the door. I let Izzie in.

She gasps. "Oh, Jess, you look lovely! You've lost so much weight — but are you okay?"

Hannah comes through the door, looking flushed. She stops for a moment. "Wow," is all she says.

It's enough.

"Are we just about ready?" I say.

We nod, but it's too early. No one will get there until later and we don't want to look too keen. Time for dancing! We turn up the speakers and start to practice our moves to Rihanna.

We don't notice the knock at the door. We don't notice anything until the flash dazzles us. We turn and see Mum in the doorway, phone in hand.

"You all look beautiful," she says quietly.

She looks at me with a kind of intensity that's embarrassing. But it's nice. For once.

But enough of the soppy stuff — who wants a moment with your mum when you could be out with your friends, getting drunk and snogging a hot boy?

"Come on!" I yell.

We go to Hannah's basement. Too many parents in my house. We dance and drink and text and post endless selfies on Instagram.

There's a rap at the door and there's Dom and Fred. They bunch together on the recliner and our pre-party goes from strength to strength. First, they're boys; second, they like us; and third, it's always better to go to a party as part of a crowd. Makes you look like the whole world is your friend.

By now we are buzzing and the boys are staring at us greedily. Any other night and I might be tempted. Either would do. But tonight, I don't want to settle for okay. Tonight, I want the strange, complicated fantasy in my head to become reality.

It's time to go. Outside, the lights begin to blur and dance as we spin down the street. Suddenly, jumping over dog poo is funny. Spinning round lampposts even funnier. I feel that Dom is close to me — never going far, breathing down my neck. Fred is tailing Hannah in the same way and Izzie is just dancing along, clearly amused.

We twist and turn along the familiar streets of our childhood. Beyond the large terraced houses, the spring air glows with the last burn of golden light and the pale blue sky arches over us. I think of the song Dad played for us at summer barbecues when I was a kid and he was still playing gigs. It always makes me think of evenings like this, of perfect summer skies and endless possibilities.

We all get the giggles as we suddenly realize that we're not sure of the number of Matt's house, but before we get around to texting anyone, we just listen out for the noise, and then we hear the bass and then we see the people ringing the doorbell, and we know that we've found the right place.

CHAPTER
TWENTY-TWO

Observation #5:

Rules are there to be broken.

There's even a bloody fountain outside! Dom wants to jump in it, but I pull him away as Izzie rings the doorbell, and then we burst through and get our first glimpse of Matt's house. It's huge — much bigger than ours. I can't believe his parents have let him have a party. Each piece of furniture looks like it's just come from an antique shop.

We girls head for the music and the front room while the boys are sent on a mission to find us drinks.

The room is pulsing with sound. My ears hurt, but my feet want to dance. There's a small group of bodies, weaving and stomping in the center of the room. Around the edge, in huge chairs and sofas, more bodies are strewn. Some are girls, entangled with each other, looking out at the action. Others are couples, all roving hands and winding tongues, eyes shut. I try to see if any are Matt, without looking like some perv who likes watching other people snog.

I can't see him anywhere. But the music is calling me and Dom grabs my hand and we start to dance. For a while, it feels like the best thing — the music pounding through me, friendly faces, Dom staring longingly. I'm happy when I dance, don't care if I'm good or bad. I'm not out to impress anyone. I just want to move and feel the beat and, for a while, that's enough.

Then someone changes the music and it gets grungy. I don't hate it, but I can't dance to it. Someone shoves a glass of something in my hand. I begin to feel a bit on edge. The glow is going off the day. Izzie is deep in debate with some guy. He's clearly teasing her but she's giving as good as she gets and they're both having a good time. Can't see Hannah, so I decide to try and find her — it gives me something to do and also gives me a chance to find Matt.

As I wander through the large hallway, I catch a glimpse of a tall blond girl with smoky eyes, a blue dress and black jeggings. It takes a second for it to sink in that it's me, my reflection, caught in a long mirror.

I pull myself together and avoid the snogging couple sitting on the telephone table, as the telephone sadly beeps to itself on the floor. They seem to be having sex with their clothes on — at least it's safe, but it looks like they're gonna get clothing burns. "Get a room," I say as I pass.

I drift into the kitchen. Cat is standing with a gaggle of tall boys around her who are taking it in turns to make her laugh. But where's Jack? Is that why she's happy, cos he's not here? It's nice, though weird, to see her laughing. I decide to give her a wide berth, but I do want a drink, so I sneak in. The kitchen's huge, so I can get to the fridge without going too near them.

"That's my sister," I hear Cat call, and I turn, unsure of what reception I'm going to get. I mean, private Cat has thawed to me a bit, but public Cat? I might still be too fat and embarrassing for her. She is smiling as she looks at me and I can detect no obvious signs of menace. The boys all are smiling, too. "So, have you made any more crazy clips lately?" one says. This seems my cue to go and talk to them, so I do.

"I think that was my fifteen minutes of fame used up there," I begin.

I quite like the next twenty minutes or so. It's like I'm in some kind of spotlight that makes life sparkly. They laugh when I retell my story. Cat listens and laughs in the right places.

The boys seem to like me, either for me being me, or because I'm Cat's sister. The surfaces in the ultra-modern kitchen are very shiny, and they act like mirrors so that I see Cat and then me.

"I need to find Hannah," I say as I edge out, but no one looks as I go. I'm invisible again.

I've done the hall, the kitchen and both downstairs rooms. I'm beginning to feel a bit down now. I could go back into the dance room and find a boy. But I'm not quite up for that. There's only one boy here for me.

I need a more chilled vibe, so I find my way through the French doors into the garden.

The cool air hits me, and instantly I relax. It's beautiful out here, though I can barely see where I'm going in the dusk. I can just pick out a white lounger and aim for that. I stretch out on it, kick back and try to pick out how many colors there are in the warm evening sky. The sun's long gone but what remains is pale green and yellow, melting into ever deepening shades of blue. I wish Hannah were here to help me name all the colors.

"Having a good time?" A voice comes out of the darkness. I peer forward. A guy slumps down on the lounger next to me.

Be still, my beating heart.

It's Matt.

"Great," I say, "but I need a minute to cool down. It's too hot in there."

"Yeah," he says companionably and then starts to roll something that looks suspiciously like a spliff. "Sent any more teachers over the edge recently?"

As I sit up and edge onto the side of the lounger, I find him sitting close to me and putting the spliff in my hand. I take it from him; our fingers meet. I can feel the warmth of his leg next to mine, and his hand now sits partially on my thigh. His shoulder presses on mine. What do you say in a situation like this? *Just get on with it and kiss me?* But I want to savor every moment.

"No, I'm pretty much a model student at the moment."

He seems to be laughing at me. Am I missing something?

"You gonna smoke that or just use it as a fashion accessory?" He gestures toward the spliff.

Embarrassed, I hand it back. "Sure, just get enough of that at home so I don't really feel the need now."

"Only the daughter of a rock star — sorry, rock twinkle — could say that." He remembered something I said. Go me!

"We celebrity kids don't need drugs to be cool," I say.

He arches an eyebrow at me. "And I do?"

Now I'm flustered. "'Course not. And spliff as a fashion accessory — that's a new idea. You could match the paper to what you're wearing. Or the color of your eyes, I suppose."

"What color do you suggest for me?" He leans in as if making it easier to see his face so that he's tantalizingly close.

"You've got brown eyes, so the fashion guide recommends that burnt umber is the shade you're after this season," I say, working as hard as I can to be lighthearted.

"You know the color of my eyes? Cute. You noticed." 'Course, I noticed.

"But what color are yours?" So, he's never noticed, but now he peers into my face. I stop talking and turn to him. He smiles and I see again exactly how perfect he is. He strokes some hair away that was falling over my face and seems to consider me closely. For a second, I think that the world has stopped. Then I remember to start breathing. No one wants to kiss a corpse. He leans in closer.

This is it, I think. Don't mess it up, this is the moment that it's all been about.

"Matt, you idiot!" a voice booms through the dark as some mountain of a boy lurches through the shadows toward us.

"Here you are," he shouts. "I've got him!" he calls back to the house. He stares cheerfully at us both, while a few others start to filter out to sit down and chat. I don't know any of them, and Matt doesn't introduce me or look at me.

I get up from the lounger, unnoticed, and go inside, invisible again. The spotlight has moved on.

In the huge, modern bathroom, I lock the door and take a minute to compose myself. As I stare at my reflection in the mirror, I can barely focus on myself. Is that me in the reflection, behind all that makeup? In my head, there's a clip going round and round of Matt's face, his lips — only a few inches from mine in the soft dusk. And then his friend calls out and he acts as if I'm not there. If I could just get him to look at me again, then maybe I'd have another chance.

For a moment, I wonder whether I'm going to be sick and, indeed, whether I should be sick. I drink as much water as I can manage and then there's someone pounding on the door. I open it and some guy runs in and spews in the bath.

I go back into the main room. Izzie is now talking to Alex. She sees me and smiles joyously. I give her the thumbs-up and wander on. After a while, I slip off. I have to see Matt. It's getting late and I can feel my time running out. I've no reason to see him after this, no reason to call round. I could message him but it's not the same.

He sat close to me — I could breathe his breath.

Back in the garden, there are just chilled bodies. I see one of the guys I was talking to earlier. "Have you seen Matt?" I ask. He shakes his head.

In the house, I can't find him anywhere. I stand at the top landing, wondering whether I can look around upstairs or not. Then I see his tall shape at the bottom of the stairs, wineglass in hand. Garden Guy walks past: "Matt, dude, how's it going?"

"Looking up, man, looking up."

"How so? Hey — that girl was looking for you."

"Which one?" Matt's distracted and looking up the stairs.

"You dog! You know — YouTube girl, Cat's sister?"

"Jess? Nice girl but ..."

"Big girl, too." Garden Guy laughs. "Well, by the look of it, she wants a piece of you. Don't think so. Her sister, now that's a very different proposition."

Matt's impatient. "You're boring me now, man. Zara's waiting for me." With this, he jumps up from stair to stair.

"Now you're talking," Garden Guy shouts. "Go get her!" I push back behind some cupboards. He bounds past and his eyes flicker in my direction, but he doesn't see me. A door opens, and Zara is framed in the doorway, smiling, a large shirt hanging off her, showing her bare shoulder and long, thin legs. She backs in, Matt follows her, the door slams shut.

It's like I was never here.

CHAPTER
TWENTY-THREE

Observation #9:
There are the things that you know you know. And the things
that you don't. And then there are the things that you suddenly
realize you knew all along, but never admitted to yourself.

I slump to the ground. My heart lies torn in rags. The words ring around me, burning in the air. *Big girl, Cat's sister, don't think so, Zara's waiting.* Upstairs now, his hands are on skinny Zara, his lips on hers. And I am crying in a corner, feeling fatter than ever before.

I feel someone sitting down next to me. Someone gives me a tissue. I look up. It's Alex. He doesn't smile or talk. He just sits there.

"Thanks," I say.

He nods; we continue sitting like this.

"I'm not really having a great time," I say.

He nods again and goes off. I can't think what to do next. I look at my phone. I'm way past my curfew. There are several messages from Mum and Dad. I'm in deep doo-doo. I don't think that I can even walk home now.

A heavy tread on the stairs. Alex again, with a glass of water. I drink it, I say thank you. I take the chance to look at him. He has Hannah's dark eyes but his hair is deep brown, not really red now that I look at him properly. He's tall and slim. I begin to see why someone might like him.

"Do you want to go home? Cos I'll take you if you do."

I nod. "But I need some fresh air first," I say.

He pulls me to my feet and pushes me up another set of the stairs. I try to blank my mind about which room Matt is in now and what he's doing to Zara or she's doing back to him.

Alex opens a door and pulls me through. I find myself on a rooftop patio, complete with seats and potted plants. We are high up, higher than the tall trees in the garden and on the street. The sky is inky black now, but stained in the distance with the orange lights of central Manchester.

I sit down on a chair and Alex pulls one close to me.

I don't feel the need to make conversation. Some stars seem to be changing color and jumping around a bit. A cool breeze hits us. I shiver but I'm glad. The whole evening, week, three weeks, have been overheated, and it's good to feel cold. It feels real.

"He's my friend, but he can be an idiot," Alex says simply. "I didn't know that you liked him. I would have said something if I had." There is a pause. "You're not his type."

I don't question what this means. I don't need to be told the subtext.

The breeze, the water, the sudden peace — all begin to calm me down. Maybe I'm too calm. Maybe I'll break down when I'm on my own. Or maybe I can just bounce back — I'm a fat girl after all, bouncy old me. Dust myself off and go back to being feisty Jess, good for a chat and a snog.

It's too late now. Hot tears begin to slide down my cheeks. I don't shake or sob but I can't stop them, even though I know my makeup will follow their course.

Alex puts his hand on mine. I don't stop crying and I don't respond.

Then he puts his arm around my shoulders and pulls me close. It feels good, his warmth and strength. My tears fall on his hand and he doesn't wipe them away.

I've known him all my life and he's never been anything but kind and funny to me. And he's here now and he's not leaving. I look up at him. He stares at me and wipes away a tear from my cheek. My makeup leaves a black stain on his finger.

"I'm a mess," I whisper. He says nothing but leans in to kiss me.

What? "No," I say and push him away. "Sorry, but no."

He pulls back like he's been electrocuted. "I'm sorry …" he begins.

"No," I say, wiping away my tears. "You're lovely. I just don't want … I don't know what I want."

A door slams. I jump up, startled.

"Jess?" It's Hannah. "Alex, what are you doing here?" Now it's my turn to leap away from him as if I've been caught with my hand in the biscuit jar. "I don't know what's going on and, frankly, I don't want to know. But Jess, you've got to come. It's Cat."

What remains of my heart starts to pound. "What's wrong?"

"Just come." She takes me by the hand and drags me down to a locked door. "She's in there. She's been awhile."

"Is she drunk?" I say.

"No." Hannah's face creases with worry. "Worse."

"What's worse than that?"

"Jack."

Of course. "What's he done now?"

"He just turned up with another girl, his ex-girlfriend, and dumped Cat in front of a whole crowd of people."

My insides burn with fury. A minute ago, I was down and out, ready to sob myself into a puddle and drown myself in my own tears. But now, that idiot is messing with my sister.

"Cat." I hammer on the door. "It's Jess."

No reply.

"Cat." I try again and listen to the door for any signs of movement. "Are you sure that she's in there?"

Hannah nods. "I chased after her when it happened." She pauses as if considering her words. "No one else went so I thought I better."

"What do you mean?"

"Well, if someone did that to you or me, we'd watch out for each other."

"Yes, and your point is?"

Hannah looks embarrassed. "Does Cat have any girlfriends?"

I look at the locked door and just the two of us standing by it. Below, in the huge stairwell, a few people are chatting and pointing, whispering behind hands. "Looks like it's just me."

I sit down next to the door. "Cat, I'm not going anywhere until you come out." Still no reply.

"Okay, so now I'm going to talk very loudly and tell all the people who can hear me about all the stupid things you have done in your life. I am going to start with the incident at the age of seven, when you did cartwheels on the school field and had forgotten that you'd not put any knickers on … I think we'll now move on to the famous incident involving …"

The door flies open. "Do you think this is funny?" Cat stands, a black figure silhouetted against the bright lights behind.

"No, I just want you out of here." I move in for a hug but she pushes me away. "Let's go, Cat."

More chatter and laughter rise up from below and Cat recoils as if touching hot metal. "They can't see me. How can I get out without being seen?"

I take her by the hand, and this time, she doesn't pull away. "I'm not going to let you run away as if you've done anything wrong. We go together with our heads held high."

"I don't think I can do that, Jess."

I hold her and she slumps against me. "How could he do this to me? In front of everyone?"

"Because he's the kind of guy who thinks it's okay to look at Mum's arse and my tits. And that's why we're going out the front. Okay?"

She sniffs. "Let me do my makeup first." I don't mention that her eyes are red and puffy and not much will cover that. I just let her get on and stroke her hair from time to time.

"Okay, let's do this."

We walk down the stairs. I try not to look upward. I try not to imagine that Matt will appear and say, "Jess, I've made a terrible mistake. It was you all along that I wanted."

He doesn't. It's just me and Cat and a few bitchy girls and mean boys who watch our progress with smiles and rolled eyes.

As we reach the front door, someone wobbles up behind. "Cat, no hard feelings, eh?"

It's Jack. Drunk, smiling, smug. "You're great but a bit too — cold. A guy needs a bit more passion in a girlfriend, if you know what I mean."

Cat is tense and shaking next to me. I snap.

"Cold? How's this for cold?" I grab a flower vase next to the front door, take out the flowers and throw the water in his face.

"You crazy bitch," he splutters.

I throw the flowers over him, for a final humiliation. Then I take Cat's hand and we walk off into the night, without a backward glance. It's only once we've got around the corner that I begin to sob.

CHAPTER TWENTY-FOUR

Observation #7:
Girls moan about pictures that make them
feel bad about their bodies. Then they slag off
every other girl's body. Girls, get a grip.

"No," Cat says, "we're not doing that. Snap out of it." She's so fierce and so sad that I stop crying, wipe away a few tears. So we trudge home in silence. Once inside, we find Dad still up, strumming a few chords, sitting in a haze of smoke.

"All right, girls?"

"All right, Dad," I lie. "I'm off to bed." Cat says nothing but just walks upstairs. Tears are welling up but I just manage to keep them under control.

"Smart," he says and then drifts back into his happy little jam session. I look back at him through the doorway, willing him to look back up, cos just now, I need someone to look after me. Part of me wants to burst into tears and tell him all about it, so he can make it all right.

But he might look at me with disappointment. I don't think I could bear that. Anyway, no one can make this all right.

So, I'm on my own. What a fool I've been. In my room the tears start falling, hot and wet. I want to take this bloody dress off but the zip's stuck. My fingers fumble as I try to get a good hold on it, but I'm too tired to even work a bloody zip.

It's like Zara's in my head now, thin and perfect, telling me everything that's wrong with me.

Stupid Jess. So fat that the zip on your dress is stuck. LMFAO.

Finally, the zip moves and I rip the dress off, throwing it on the floor. It lies there, a symbol of all that's gone wrong tonight. All that preparation, all that hope … I think bitterly of how excited I was only a few hours ago.

What were you thinking? A girl like you, and Matt?

I think about the last few weeks and how rubbish they have been. All the headaches, stomachaches, the bad moods, the constant hunger: all for a door to open. All for Matt to walk past me toward Zara's smiling face.

You think you're so smart, don't you, Jess. You think you're different, superior to us normal girls. Well, look where it got you. Face it, you've got life wrong — you and your crazy gran. Girls are judged on the way they look, and you fail on every level.

I lie curled on my bed, replaying the evening over and over again.

Matt liked me, he did, but I can't compete with girls who look like Zara. They might be shallow, they might be mean. But they're hot. And I'm a fat loser freak. Who has just got everything wrong.

And it's no consolation that Alex seems to like me. I mean, what was that?

He felt sorry for me, that's all. And anyway … Alex? I mean, he's not exactly gonna be in a boy band, is he?

I sob into my pillow, pulling the duvet over my head, as if somehow this will protect me from the outside world. But how can I protect me from myself? The sky is light by the time I drift off into uneasy sleep.

When I wake up in the morning, there's a glorious moment when I don't think of anything, but then it all comes back to me.

I know it's a bit of a cliché but my heart is broken. I never thought that it really happened — that your heart feels real pain. But no, it's true. My chest hurts, like there's physical damage in there.

My phone beeps, but I don't want to see anything on it. Unless … unless … Has Matt come to his senses? My heart lurches as I pick up the phone.

But it's not his name on the display. It's Alex. I can't talk to him yet.

I try to make a start on sorting out my thoughts and feelings.

Okay, so I tried to be a "perfect" girl, whatever that is. I made myself lose weight for a guy. For three weeks, I starved myself, I had the make-over, the dress. I did look different. And for what?

Either being perfect isn't for me, or being perfect isn't what it's made out to be.

And how does that leave me feeling about Matt? The bruise in my chest throbs particularly intensely at the thought of him. Yesterday, I would have lain down in a puddle and let him walk over me. A few seconds ago, I was desperate for it to be him. But I have to think this through. He's the kind of guy who chooses Zara over me. He prefers a girl who bullies others. Clearly, he's not the guy for me. But someone needs to tell that to my heart.

At least my humiliation is private. Cat's heart was thrown to the lions in front of everyone. Izzie and Hannah will pick me up and put together the pieces. But Cat has no one that I know of … apart from me.

I drag myself out of bed. I walk the few steps across the landing from my room to Cat's. I knock on the door.

No reply.

I knock again. "Cat?"

Is there movement inside?

Now I'm getting worried. I push open the door. It's quiet and dark in here. The familiar Audrey Hepburn posters on the wall. The copies of *Vogue* neatly piled on the table.

A small lump under the duvet reassures me that at least she's not gone missing.

"Cat?" I repeat.

The lump moves.

The lump makes some kind of noise.

I take a few steps into the room.

"Go away."

"No."

I wait. Only silence.

"Are you okay?"

"No."

"Then I'm not going away."

I sit in the chair next to her bed and pick up a book and start to read. The duvet reveals Cat, staring.

"What are you doing?" she asks.

"I just wanted to make sure that you're all right."

She looks at me hard. "I'm fine."

"I'm sorry about Jack."

She bristles. "I don't want to talk about it." But she's not finished yet. "But you're not sorry. You hated him."

"I hate him worse now. I thought he was a knob before but that was downright cruel."

She starts to go back under the duvet. "I told you. I don't want to talk about it. I'll be fine."

I feel my bottom lip start to wobble. "Well, anyway, I'm not fine."

"Oh."

"Do you want to know why?"

Just silence. I want to scream at her but I try and keep it all together.

"Cat, I'm such an idiot."

"I could have told you that." There might be a hint of a smile on her lips.

"Don't be mean."

"Are you crying?" she says in surprise.

"Yes," I say, wiping away the tears.

"Oh." There you go — Cat, queen of the monosyllable.

"Is that all you can say?"

Cat leans back in bed. "Why don't you go and eat something, Jess? That's what you normally do when you're upset."

Ouch. That really hurts. "That's not fair," I reply.

She purses her lips into her usual pout. "Might not be fair, but it would be true."

At that point, our old friend Silence fills the room again.

I'm the first to break it. "Can I ask you one question?"

"Okay."

I steel myself. We never talk about important stuff and I'm not sure how she will react. "Are you hungry all the time?"

After a short pause, she answers. "Yes."

"And doesn't that drive you mad?"

A cold smile crosses her face. "Yes."

"Then why do you do it?"

There is a longer pause now, but she's not chucked me out yet.

"Because I looked in the mirror and I didn't like the way I looked. So, I did something about it."

"And now?"

"I still hate what I look like."

"But you're so pretty! Everyone thinks so!"

"My nose — I hate the shape of my nose. And my forehead — it's so big."

I stare at my sister's perfect face.

But she's off now. I've never heard her speak so much and with so much feeling. She's listing all these minor imperfections. Her freckles, the moles on her arms, the slight bump on her nose, her wonky eyebrows — it's like she's possessed. I suddenly see how she sees the world. She feels endlessly judged and so she judges me and every other girl in the world.

"But Cat, you're beautiful."

She laughs hollowly. "Then why did Jack dump me? That's the deal, isn't it — a girl has to look perfect and then everything else will be all right?" She looks almost desperate now.

"I tried being perfect for a bit but I don't think it's going to work for me," I say sadly.

I tell her about Matt and then the moment with Alex.

"Well, what did you expect? Matt and you … I tried to warn you. He collects adoring girls. He just loves to be loved. But he only goes out with the trophy girls." She considers what I said for a moment. "Alex is pretty cool. He's not hot. You could do worse. I mean, it's about time you had a proper boyfriend."

"I don't know if I like him or not." Cat makes that face again. I hear her stomach growl.

"Let me make you some lunch, Cat. Whatever you like."

A thought suddenly strikes me. "You've always liked my white chocolate and raspberry cake."

The corner of her mouth twitches. "Do you know how long I'll have to exercise to work that off?"

"Surely, today of all days, you deserve something that makes you feel good even if it's just for a few minutes."

She doesn't reply.

"That's it then, I'm making it."

An hour later, I'm back at the door with two bowls and a perfect dessert. I sniff it and I think my olfactory system is about to explode.

I tap on the door and go in. Cat's still in bed but she's sitting up rather than slumped between the covers.

"Shove up then," I say.

She looks at me as if I have two heads.

"Make room for me," I say and gesture to the bed as well as I can when my hands are so full.

"You want to get into my bed? When I'm still in it?"

I plonk myself down on the bed and cut her a large slice of dessert. "Okay, so you've taught me how to do sit-ups, burpees, mountain-climbers, etc. I am going to train you in the art of having fun. So, this is how it works. We snuggle up ..."

Cat recoils like there's a tarantula in the room. "I am not snuggling up with anyone. I do not snuggle."

I stare at her sadly. "Maybe that's a step too far. How do you feel about my shoulder touching yours?"

She gives it some thought. "That might be acceptable."

"Okay." I peel back her duvet as she stares at me with suspicion. "So, this is how I hang out with my friends. First, we sit in close proximity." I lean back next to her and I can almost feel her twitching.

"Okay? How's that?"

"It's weird but just about bearable."

I hand her a bowl. "Then we eat. Try it."

Cat takes the smallest bite imaginable.

"Try again. How's that?"

She takes a deep breath.

"Well?"

Cat pauses. "It's all right."

"All right? It's bloody well more than all right. Go on, this is one day when you can say what you really think. How do you feel when you eat it?"

She takes a full spoonful this time and savors it. Her face seems to soften. "How do I feel? Glorious."

She starts to smile as I find myself grinning, too. I still have a raw place in my chest but I smile and feel the pain at the same time. "I'll take glorious. And now, for the final step …"

"What's that?"

"We watch Netflix. How do you feel about *Gilmore Girls*?"

"Who are they?"

I look at her in disappointment. "Oh, Cat. You have so much to learn. Now lean back, eat and enjoy."

And that's how we spend the afternoon.

CHAPTER TWENTY-FIVE

Invisible Rule #16:
Girls are supposed to show more emotion than they feel;
boys are supposed to hide all the emotion that they feel.

So, that's all rather nice. It is good beyond ANYTHING to eat again without feeling stressed about calories or losing weight. But nothing else is okay.

My phone buzzes on and off all day. Every time I snatch it up, thinking it will show Matt's name in glowing letters. But it never is him. I spend hours reviewing the gig. The rehearsal. How right his skin felt the few times I touched it. How he stared into my eyes and laughed long and hard at what I said. But then, like a video clip I can't erase no matter how hard I try, there's Zara, standing in the open door. In the end, I turn to what generally cheers me up: food. I skim through all my old posts about the great things that I've cooked and see which one has the most likes.

I see one of my last ones — my favorite. The school made from gingerbread. It was only a few weeks ago, but it feels like a different girl posted that. Underneath it, my stupid comment. #thegirlwhoeatslife. More like the girl who's eaten by life at the moment.

My thumb twitches as if to swipe ever onward but I'm drawn back to it. How did I feel when I wrote that? Well, great, in fact. Okay, I was angry at school and Mum. But at least I knew who I was.

Maybe the old Jess wasn't so bad after all? She certainly liked herself more.

My phone buzzes but I turn it off. It's just tormenting me now. Nothing good is going to come from that phone today.

But tomorrow, I'm going to start making happier choices and then I'll see what happens to my battered heart.

Next morning, it's dark and wet outside, so I stay in bed as long as is humanly possible.

Mum stands outside my room and hollers.

Then the door shuffles open and small footsteps whisper over the floor.

Mum's played her key card — Lauren.

The light blazes on.

"I can't see you," Lauren says.

"Turn off the light," I say, "it hurts my eyes."

"You should go to the doctor's then," she says. "You're not normal. You must be part girl, part vampire."

I pull the duvet over my head.

Like a trained torturer, she rips it back. She's four — how did she learn all this?

"You are annoying," I say.

Her bottom lip sticks out and it starts to quiver.

Tears start to roll down her cheeks. "Alice doesn't love me, and now you."

I can't take any more. "Okay," I say, "I give in." I sit up. I mean, I'm not going to sleep now, am I?

And with that, she leads me downstairs as she shouts in triumph, "I got her up!"

In the kitchen, there's an amazing sight. Cat is eating breakfast. Well, if you call a small selection of fruit *breakfast,* but even, this is the first time she's been seen eating before twelve p.m. in a long while. Even Mum seems happy.

"Due to the intervention of the world's most annoying child, I might have time for fluffy pancakes if anyone wants them?" I say.

Mum looks tempted. "I am doing Body Combat followed by Ultimate Spin so perhaps I can have half of one."

"Knock yourself out and have a whole one," I say. "Cat?"

"A very small one."

"I shall make you a pancake only visible under a microscope."

And off I go, whisking and whipping, and after a while, when everyone is around the table eating food, an old feeling just flickers up inside me. A moment of happiness. Just a twinkle, mind. But it's there. That is enough to get me dressed and out the house for school.

But I don't climb the small hill that leads me to St. Ethelreda's with any enthusiasm. I refused to text or join any group chats about the party. As far as I'm concerned, I'd like to just delete it from history. I know Sana and Bex will want to hear every detail, but I'm not sure I can bear to go through it all again. And then there's that little bit of drama that only two people know about. Alex and me. I'm definitely keeping that one to myself for the moment. Think I'll stick to exams and cooking.

Sure enough, as soon as I walk through the form room door, they crowd around me.

"Tell us everything. I've heard so many different stories."

"Did Jack really dump Cat?"

"Did you really throw water all over Jack?"

I take a deep breath. "I was merely acting in accordance with concepts of universal justice."

Hannah picks up my theme. "You mean it's a truth universally acknowledged that idiot boys need to be doused in water?"

"Something like that," I say.

Izzie asks, "How's Cat? Do you want me to do a healing potion for her?"

"She's had some of my pancakes today. That's healing enough," I return. "She'll be okay. She's best rid of him. He really didn't treat her well."

Bex is all big eyes. "At least she's had a boyfriend though. Even if he was a rubbish one."

I have to shut this down. "No. I think he's really hurt her."

Hannah backs me up. "You should have seen him. He just turned up with his ex draped round him. They were practically having sex in the kitchen in front of everyone, and Cat walked in."

"She didn't know before?" Izzie asks.

The old guilt turns in my stomach. "I had a suspicion. But that was all. I didn't know for sure."

"Would you have said something?" Sana says.

I shrug. "I like to think that I would. I would now. But at the time, I didn't want to make her mad with me. We've only just started talking again."

After a small silence, Bex says, "I saw a photo of Zara and Matt looking very close."

"I missed that," I say as lightly as I can. "But yeah, they seemed to go off together. Make a very good-looking couple." I can feel Hannah's and Izzie's sympathy but I don't want it. "Sorry, Bex, I didn't snog him for you. Seems like I'm not his type."

"Such a waste though." Sana sniffs. "You can have the personality of a sewer rat, but if you're good-looking, you get the boy."

"I think you're being a bit rude to sewer rats, aren't you?" I say. "What have they ever done to you?"

The bell goes and propels us off and out to our various lessons, and I take a deep breath. I can just drift through this day.

At home time, I lean against a tree full of blossoms, waiting for Hannah to walk home with. She's deep in conversation about satire in early nineteenth-century novels, so I could be here awhile. My phone buzzes and it's Imogen's name that lights up the screen. She wants to go shopping with me! Now that is something to think about. I start to plan my witty response.

Then Zara is here, all hair and smiles, surrounded by her posse. There's a screech of tires and the revving of an engine. A dark red Mini squeals to a halt next to them and a door swings open.

I've been in that Mini. I've sat with my hand so close to its driver's I nearly passed out.

Maybe I should hate Zara even more now. But I don't, I realize. I don't hate Matt either.

If someone chooses her over me, then there's something wrong with them, not me.

I know that. I just don't always feel it.

I can't choose my feelings but I can focus on the positive. After all, I was — or I am — the girl who eats life.

So, that's what I'm going to do.

Devour life up.

I start to text Imogen. Maybe new clothes will be a fresh start.

CHAPTER TWENTY-SIX

Observation #101:
What if you're a girl and you'd rather read a book than
shop — do you get expelled from Girl Club?

I survive the week and I'm off with my new best friend, Imogen. Okay, this does feel a bit weird. She's older than me and I only really know her from her blog. Yet here I am, getting ready to meet her. It's like the "before" of a bad Internet safety campaign message. I can almost hear the teacher now. *So, boys and girls, can we see where this poor unfortunate girl went wrong? Yes, sir, she met someone from the Internet and now she's dead.* But that's not my greatest fear. No. I seem to have learned nothing recently, as my greatest fear is what to wear. I mean, she's a fashion blogger. But I refuse to be beaten. They are just clothes. Inanimate objects. I am a conscious, sentient human who is clearly in control.

I look at the pile of clothes on my bed and whimper.

My phone pings. It's Alex. My heart lurches a bit. Another awkward thing. He's texted before but I just ignored it. I don't know what to say. When I look at the message, I have no idea what he's up to.

There are four photos. And each one is of weirdly arranged food.

Well, not all of it. There's a close-up of a Polo mint. Then what looks like the letter *K* made from breadsticks. A close-up of the *R* from the wrapper of a Rolo packet. And a *U* made from peas. Yes, peas. *K, R, U* and … oh, the Polo is an *O*.

R U O K

Are you okay? I can't help but smile. I mean, he's the first person to ask me for a while. I send a GIF back of a smiley face and a thumbs-up. It's not personal but it's sort of true. And then I realize that I am smiling in real life. I check in the mirror. Yep, there it is — the smile is now creeping across my face. Right, clothes, this is ridiculous, I think. I can take you on.

After a few goes, I've chosen something I feel happy in. I check my reflection in the mirror and you know what? It looks okay. Not amazing but okay. No ridiculous makeup, no high-maintenance hair. Just me.

A few hours later, I'm not just smiling, I'm actually laughing. Imogen and I are sitting in my favorite café where hipster dudes with man buns and multiple piercings are serving us the best coffee ever brewed. I have a few bags of shopping next to me, full of clothes hand-picked by Imogen. We're competing to see who's done the most stupid thing trying to lose weight.

"One day, I just drank green tea. By the end of it, I was hallucinating and my tongue tasted like a sewage farm."

"I tried some meal replacement and was so hungry I almost ate the packet that the powder came in. In the end, I ate a muffin and felt much better."

All of a sudden, Imogen leans forward. "It's entirely up to you, and I get that the whole 'Fat Girl vs. Mean Girl' thing upset you. But I think you should write a post for my blog. It would be good to get a different voice out there."

Old uncertainties surface. "But I'd feel a fraud being on your blog. I mean, I've spent a few miserable weeks trying to reduce. I don't know what I've got to say. And even if I did have something to say, why would anyone want to listen to me?"

"Because you're cool, Jesobel. And you've had the experience of going viral. And you're Steve Jones's daughter. All those things. But most of all because I think all girls, in fact all women, probably feel like you a lot of the time. I know I do."

I stir the last bit of my coffee. "But you're weird like me. And I mean it as a compliment."

She clinks mugs with me. "My life goal is weird. Cheers to weird."

Then my phone goes again. "I just want to read this, sorry," I say. It's from Alex again.

How do you avoid a soggy bottom?

I smile. I text back before I have a chance to think about it.

What are you making?

Imogen says, "Jess, sorry, but I think I have to go now."

I look up. "Okay, well, I really enjoyed this. Thank you for your help with the clothes. Who knew that there were shops that I could go in and not feel embarrassed about needing bigger sizes?"

"Think about what I said. My blog needs you."

I laugh it off as we hug and then she's gone. But I'm not alone, as my phone pings again. I walk back to the tram stop to get back home, and as I go, I'm accompanied by regular updates from Alex. Is he really baking? *Ping.*

A chicken pie. Something manly. I'm making it for you.

You need to bake it blind.

WTF???

Oh dear. You have much to learn.

Any chance of a tutorial?

And then he sends a picture. Well, I can't help but LOL. Which is slightly embarrassing as I'm now standing, waiting for the tram.

At least three complete strangers turn around to look at me. In the photo is the worst excuse for a pie I've ever seen in my life. It's gray, with gravy seeping out from several gaping cracks on the top, and it's broken down the side.

But he made it for me.

Presentation seems to be an issue.

But taste is everything, isn't it?

I can't taste it in a photo.

True. You may never get to experience this one. Such a shame.

My face is splitting from side to side.

By the time the tram hums back to my stop, I'm glowing. I practically skip back home. My soul skips, anyway. My feet just walk in a more acceptably cool fashion. I like to be different, but there has to be a limit.

Within a few minutes, I'm very glad that I kept my skipping under control. There's a tall figure standing opposite my house. Definitely male, on the rather skinny side. He straightens up when he sees me. If I had skipped up the road, I don't think he would have actually minded.

"Hey," I say.

"Hey back," he says.

In his hands is a small plastic box. In the box is a small, gray pie. Alex regards it sadly.

"I won't ask you to try it," he says. "It's too embarrassing."

"It's okay," I say. "It might taste all right."

He shakes his head. "I wouldn't bet on it."

I take the box from him. His fingers and mine graze past each other. I'm too nervous to look up directly at him.

Instead, I poke the pie. I break a bit off and taste. I chew thoughtfully.

"It's very … manly," I say.

And then I start to choke, laughing.

"Seriously," I say when I can speak, "this is the most masculine pie

I have ever tasted. I am almost overwhelmed by the maleness of this pie."

He makes a face. "The words *masculine* and *pie* just don't go together, do they?"

I eat another piece. "It's not bad. But you need to keep your hands cold when you're making the pastry. And don't mix it for so long next time." I chew and then nod. "Actually, it tastes okay. Is that cloves in the sauce?"

"Little smelly bits of wood?" he replies.

"That's the ones," I say. "I love cloves." For a second, I think what a stupid thing that is to say. Who in the history of the world has ever said, "I love cloves." But Alex doesn't laugh at my food obsession. I really think that he likes me. Not thinner, or smarter, or older, or more fashionable me. Just me.

"What's up?" Alex says. "You look like someone's eaten your last truffle."

"That would be the end of days," I say. "No, I'm fine."

A silence fills the space between us, not awkward, just there. Like there's too much to be said. Alex knows I liked Matt. Shame burns up inside me. Now that I can see a bit more clearly and I'm not driven mad by hormones, it is obvious that Alex is so much nicer than Matt. But silly, superficial me just saw the hair, the cheekbones and that smile.

Alex stands in front of me, pie in hand.

"Fancy some cake?" I say.

"Best offer I've had all day," Alex says and he follows me into the house.

CHAPTER TWENTY-SEVEN

Invisible Rule #55:
Adverts for periods must only show women wearing white shorts.
Nothing red must ever appear. But we all know the truth …

Inside, a small shadow launches itself at me. "Jess, you've got to save me. Alice is very, very cross and she won't talk to me." Lauren has attached herself to my leg and I haul her along the hall as I walk.

"Don't worry, squirt, she'll soon come around."

Her face is squashed with concern so that she resembles a raisin. "But she won't let me watch my show and I'm going to miss it." She suddenly realizes that I'm not alone. Looking up at Alex, she announces, "You are very tall and very ginger. Are you half giant?"

Embarrassment fires through me. "Lauren, you can't talk to people like that."

"You mean I'm not supposed to tell the truth? You always tell me to tell the truth though."

"It's okay." Alex bends down to Lauren. "Can you keep a secret?"

Lauren stares up at him, her eyes enormous with interest.

"I'm only a quarter giant. Which is handy sometimes. Do you want me to have a word with this Alice?"

To my amazement, Lauren takes him by the hand. She nods and points toward the living room. "She's hiding behind the sofa."

Alex looks quizzically at me and I make my best Please Humor My Little Sister expression.

"Alice?" he says.

Silence.

"Lauren wants to watch her program and you must let her."

Lauren jumps up and down with glee. "Ha! I have a quarter giant on my side so you just need to do what you're told." With that, she grabs the remote off the table and keeps it close to her chest. "I don't care if you don't like it, I'm watching *Sherlock*."

Alex and I share a smile as I suddenly feel nervous. Why am I feeling nervous in my own house?

"I think I've earned that cake now. I'm practically turning into a skeleton in front of you. For an evening of studying, I need sustenance from the girl who eats life."

"I haven't felt much like the girl who eats life lately," I confess, "but I do have cake, which I am always happy to share."

As I cut through the cake (yes, I'm baking again), my hand begins to tremble a bit. I stare at it in confusion. What is going on with me?

"What's bothering you?"

"Oh," I say breezily, "nothing much." Diverting attention from my wobbly hand, I say, "I met this girl called Imogen today. Well, more like a grown-up. She's a fashion student and she blogs about that and, well" — I don't want to refer to my size but then Alex has eyes and he knows what I look like — "being a larger girl and finding clothes. She's asked me to write a blog post but I don't know what to do."

He stares at me intently. "What do you want to do?"

"I'm not sure. Part of me wants to. But after that whole YouTube thing, I've had enough of myself plastered all over the Internet. And then ..."

"Then?"

"I'm not sure what I'd say," I end lamely.

Alex laughs so that crumbs fly out of his mouth. "Great cake by the way." He picks up the debris. "Since when do you not have something to say?"

Since I stopped eating. Since I thought I was in love with Matt.

I push some bits of cake around on my plate. "I've not been myself recently. And anyway, I promised the headmaster I wouldn't do anything else to embarrass the school. He practically made me swear to behave myself on social media."

"He can't stop you. The Jess I know would call that censorship."

He's right. I do think that.

I sigh. "I just don't want to get into any more trouble, I suppose."

Alex shakes his head. "It's one little blog. The only reason not to do it is because you don't want to. Otherwise, you're just being scared. You're Jesobel Jones, the girl who eats life."

"Maybe," I say, "but don't talk to ME about being scared." I think of something. "I'll write the blog when you sing in public."

The smile suddenly goes from his face.

"Gotcha," I say smugly. "It's not so easy, is it?"

"Okay," Alex says, "let's do a deal. If I sing in public, then you have to write an honest, personal account of what it's like to be you."

"Honest?"

"Completely."

"Personal?"

"Totally."

Okay, I'm scared. Seeing my fat legs going viral was one thing. To reveal my thoughts to the world, even if they don't read them, is a new level of scary.

"Maybe," I say. "Have some more cake while I think about it."

Alex shakes his head. "I'm full but thanks." He nods toward the living room. "Quite a sister you've got there."

"I know, what with her and Gran, I sometimes think I'm the only normal person here."

"So, I know that your gran lives here but I don't know the rest of the story," Alex says.

"What do you mean?" I say, turning the kettle on. It really is time for tea.

"I mean, why does she not go out?"

I pause. That is a very good question and I don't know the answer. "She used to. I remember we'd go all over when I was little." To protests, museums, the best cafés.

"So, when did it change?"

I try to think. "A while back. Maybe a few years ago." Things begin to click into place. "A few of her friends died around the same time. It was about then, I think."

"Do you ever try to get her out and about?"

"I did. We all did, apart from Mum. But Gran always turned us down, so after a while, we stopped trying, I guess."

Now Alex is looking at me in a way that suggests I am not perfect.

"You think we should have tried more." I try to hide my irritation.

He shrugs. "It's not for me to say. But I don't think it sounds like the best arrangement."

Anger gets the best of me. "We can't make her. And what do you know? Yes, you want to be a doctor, but I don't think you're qualified just yet."

Alex puts his hands up in submission. "You're right. But can I come with you when you take the tea up? I'd like to meet your legendary grandmother."

This is highly unusual. Hannah and Izzie sometimes go up and chat but that's about it. But his words bother me, because they hit a sore point.

"Okay," I say, "you can get the doors." So, together we climb up the creaking stairs to the warm fug of Gran's room. I knock on the door and call, "It's me, Gran. I've got a friend with me who wants to meet you. It's Alex, Hannah's brother." I push the door open and enter with Alex bending down behind me to avoid hitting his head on the sloping eaves of the room.

"Good afternoon, young man." Gran's crisp syllables cut through the smoke. "I see you share your sister's coloring. Always thought she was a very handsome girl. You're not as pretty but you have a kind face." Yes, he does.

Alex sits down where Gran points. "What amazing artwork," he says. "Yours, I take it?"

Gran waves his words away. "I had some talent once. Now I just do a few daubs to keep myself entertained." And they chat on as if they're old friends.

I try to see Gran as Alex must, how her clothes are too big for her, how her rings spin on her twig-like fingers. In the corner, there are empty bottles of diverse spirits. I love my gran and I think she is the coolest person, the freest person, I know, but now it all seems a bit squalid. Have we let her down?

After a while, she looks tired. I touch her on the hand. "I'll see Alex out now. Do you want anything else?" Her tea is cold.

"No, my darling, I'll just have a little sleep. Goodbye, young man. You may visit again if you like. It is pleasant to see a new face from time to time."

As we get downstairs, I turn to Alex, who is silent behind me. "Okay, you're right. I need to do something. But I don't know what."

"Talk to your parents."

I give him a stare. "You've met them. If something needs doing, then it's down to me."

It is.

In the hall, all sorts of feelings are whirling around inside me. We're standing as close as we did the other night. But he doesn't lean down to kiss me.

"I've got practice," he says, but this time he doesn't ask me to go.

"Okay," I say, "I'll see you sometime?" I say it like a question as I want him to offer to meet up. A coffee? Anything.

"Sure," he says and then he's gone.

I don't want him to go, but it's too late now. I had my moment at the party and I missed it because I was too obsessed with Matt.

Of all the stupid things I've done lately, this is the worst.

There was a boy right before me, a lovely, funny, smart, talented boy who really liked me for just being me.

And I've let him just walk away.

CHAPTER
TWENTY-EIGHT

Observation #21:
Sometimes food is not the answer.
But not very often.

In my room, I walk around and around. It's not a big room so this feels pretty stupid. Then I throw myself on the bed. Then I hate myself even more. I'm a walking cliché. I'll be punching a pillow yet or eating my own body weight in luxury ice cream before you know it.

But my mind's in a loop. I always have something to say in general. I am known for Having an Opinion. But just then, it wasn't that words failed me. No, they shriveled and died on my tongue. Turned to ashes. There must have been something that I could have said. *Let's go for a coffee. I'm making some great tapas — why don't you try them? I like you; you like me. Let's cut the crap and kiss.* I could have just held his hand and looked into his eyes.

But I just let him walk away.

I'm boiling in my own frustration. What do I normally do to calm down? Cook? That just doesn't seem right for once. My trainers are gleaming next to my bed and suddenly I find myself putting them on. It appears that I'm going for a run. Something's going to explode soon so I take myself out and start to pound the pavement.

The first good thing I notice is how much fitter I am than I was. Once, my lungs would have been on fire, but now I can keep going without too much trouble. The second good thing is that my leg muscles don't seem to complain as much as they used to do. And third, I'm out in the daylight on my own and feeling okay at being in public doing exercise.

That's when the bad thing happens.

I'm starting to get a bit sweaty now as I decide to take on a smallish hill. A car beeps at me and then slows down. "Oy, fatty, watch out or you'll break the pavement." Then the two guys in the car roar with laughter and disappear in a squeal of tires.

Fatty? Pavement breaker?

Charming.

It's not that I'm bothered about being perfect but that's just rude. I find my legs going even faster to try to match the pace of my heart. I can't help checking over my shoulder in case they come back. I hate myself for it but they've achieved what they wanted. I don't feel at home out here. I just want to be safe behind my own doors.

It takes a long hot shower to sort me out. And then making some cookies. During this time, I decide what to do. Okay, I'm probably never going to get through to idiots like that but I can still do *something.* Back in my room, I throw on my oldest, comfiest clothes and pin up my wet hair. I sit down at my laptop and the words just start to flow. I check and double-check my words until it's somewhere close to what I want to say.

And then I find Imogen's email address and hit send.

This is what I write.

The F-Word — Thoughts of the Rebel with a Cupcake

My name is Jesobel Jones and I am fat.

Not curvy or plump. Fat.

I'm not supposed to describe myself that way because being fat is the worst thing you can say about a person. But I don't think that. Apparently I think something that's a bit radical. Something that is unthinkable. Unsayable. I don't really care what a person looks like. What matters to me most is this — are they kind, clever, talented, great at maths, help old grannies cross the road? But it seems all that is irrelevant. All that matters, especially for a girl, is how thin she is and does she look hot in a bikini.

I'm supposed to think that the smaller I am, the less there is of me, the better. There's supposed to be a journey for fat people. You see it on TV commercials for weight loss products. In them, fat people live in black-and-white BEFORE. And then, they magically lose weight and their lives become all full of color. They smile, they fall in love, they marry. And the best bit of all, they can wear a bikini. Because you can only win at life if you can wear a bikini with pride.

That's just one stereotype about fat people but there are loads more. I know that some of you are thinking, "I bet she eats loads of fast food." Nope. Maybe once or twice a year. Probably less than you.

Or maybe you're thinking, "She's so lazy. I bet she never works out." Just came back from a 5K run. I might be fat but my lungs work fine, thank you very much.

Another thing you might wonder is, "How can she look at herself and feel okay? I mean, she's disgusting." Well, I did go through a phase when I thought like that. And sometimes I look in the mirror and I don't like what looks back, and sometimes I do. Just like everyone else. Because this is something I've realized recently. You can lose weight. You can exercise until you throw up or pass out. You can fit into a smaller dress size. It might make you happier. But then again, it might not.

I look around at the people I know, and I hate to break it to you, but thin people are miserable, too, sometimes. Thin people can have low self-esteem. Being thin isn't some magic fix to all life's troubles. You still might not like your Instagram pictures. The environment is still going to hell in a handcart. It's not going to boost your scores in tests. It just means you're a bit smaller. End of.

As I mentioned before, I go running. Yes, fat people can run. They don't cause earthquakes the moment they start to move. But today, as I ran down the street, someone yelled at me from a car, "Oy, fatty, watch out or you'll break the pavement."

Great.

Cos if you want someone to lose weight, the best thing to do is insult them. But funnily enough, that didn't work. I didn't stop and think, "Oh, some random person who I don't know and don't care much for has told me I'm fat. I must do something about that now."

Because this might come as news to you, Random Person, but I already know I'm fat.

You know what else? I went home and baked a batch of ginger and sultana cookies and ate them all. Because when I'm sad, I eat. I also eat when I'm happy.

Because food is wonderful. Food brings people together and puts smiles on their faces. Think of a birthday party without food or a cake. Think of Christmas without a turkey. What would be the point?

Food is not the enemy.

People are.

If you don't like how someone looks, maybe keep it to yourself. There's an idea. How someone else looks is nothing to do with you at all.

Nothing.

Nada.

My name is Jesobel Jones but you can call me the Rebel with a Cupcake. Yes, I'm fat. And that's okay with me.

CHAPTER TWENTY-NINE

Invisible Rule #99:
Some boys love cheesy pop but they have to
pretend that it's all about the grungy rock.

You know that you've gone viral for a second time when you have to turn your notifications off at three in the morning because otherwise you're not going to get any sleep. After that awful, yawning silence, the first "like" came. A while later the retweets started. Then the messages started coming through, and on the whole, people were going, Yes, Rebel with a Cupcake, you go girl. It's hard to describe my sense of relief. I said something. And people listened.

When some of the haters came online, I turned my phone off, but I snatched it up at dawn. Was that it? Had my post stopped spreading?

No. Thousands of retweets and likes. The Rebel with a Cupcake was going strong, striding out across the world, spreading a touch of light and joy as she went.

Strange to be eating breakfast and no one there knowing that my words were racing all around the globe.

"Why are you smiling?" Lauren asked. "Or do you have gas?"

"It's called being happy," I say. "You should ditch Alice and try it."

Her face crumples again. "You are mean to Alice. Alice doesn't like you."

"I don't think she likes you, for that matter," I fire back.

"You sound like Gran and I don't like Gran," Lauren announces as she dips her banana in the chocolate spread jar.

Mum sighs. "Oh, Jess, can you take her breakfast up? I've got a detoxing cleanse booked and I'm in a rush."

"You do know that detoxing has no medical benefits? You could just eat lots of bran."

Mum shudders at the thought. "Jess, I know your thoughts on detoxing but my nutritionist …" She's off again. I know I'm on a losing battle but there you go. As I get Gran's breakfast ready, my mood dips a bit. Mum can't be bothered to go and see Gran; Lauren dislikes her. There's something quite bad at the heart of this family. If I didn't go up, would anyone else even bother? It bothers me as I stomp upstairs.

"Don't stomp, Jesobel," Mum yells, "you are not a wildebeest."

I just stomp even more.

"Hey, Gran." I push open the door and am met with the usual fug of smoke and stale air. As I get no response, I try again. "Gran?" She mutters in her chair because, yet again, she's not slept in her bed. There's an empty, used glass beside her and also a beautiful but unfinished sketch of a woman's face. I put the toast and tea next to her. Should I stay? Should I wake her? I look around the room. It seems such a small place for such a big soul to spend a life in. I'm running late for school but I'm torn. I could just sit with her until she wakes up, but then, I need to keep school on my side.

I'm not sure if the post breaches the agreement I made. I've not mentioned the school or anyone at the school, so I really don't see what they could be upset by. But they're teachers, so therefore they can be upset by the most minute things. Like being one second late. Or a hair bobble that's not in school colors. Or the wearing of nail varnish, which obviously saps our intelligence, making us unable to think.

Gran continues to mumble. I take her hand. I can feel the soft, fast pulse of her blood under her papery skin. Same as normal. I'm beginning to feel that I need to challenge what goes on as normal in this house. With that thought, I head off to school.

The highlight of the day is seeing Zara's face as I walk into the dining hall at lunchtime and a spontaneous round of applause breaks out. "Loved the post, Jess" and other nice comments are made. I get hugs from lots of my favorite people and nasty stares from others. But hey, I can take the hate. Zara looks like she's swallowed a lemon at the same time as a rubbish truck has dumped loads of rotting fish next to her. "Who does she think she is?" she hisses. "Like anyone cares what she says." Lara, Tara, Tilly and Tiff vigorously nod in agreement. I just smile the biggest smile I can. Being happy really winds up people who hate you. It's the best revenge.

The rest of the day is uneventful, really, if you call Destiny Snow punching Aisha Chaudhry in the face for copying her homework "uneventful." But in this place, copying work is a bit like drowning a kitten. You just don't do it. As I walk home, I begin to think about life beyond school. All being well, I'll get the grades to go to sixth form college. A new start, new people. Perhaps the teachers will be a bit less crazy there. Perhaps respect and free speech will be encouraged. I might as well believe in a magical land being hidden at the back of a wardrobe.

Back at home, I wander round the house in a state of discontent. Yes, my post has gone well, but strangely, the joy wears off quite quickly. I head into the wilderness reserve that passes for a garden at the back of our house. There's a lawn hiding somewhere out there and even, so the legends say, a summerhouse. But even though it's a mess, it's a late spring glorious mess, with trees gently swaying in the breeze as rays of sun dance, dappled, across the long grass of the lawn. It's lovely. I stare up at Gran's window and think of her staring out.

Enough is enough. Time to make things happen around here. I enlist the reluctant help of Lauren and Alice. "Take whatever you want from the house but make it beautiful."

"Anything?" Lauren quizzes me. "I can bring the fridge out?"

"If the cord reaches, yes, but I was thinking more of all the cushions and throws. Let's just make it very pretty."

At this point, Cat drifts by. "Have you gone mad?" Admittedly, I'm currently draping Christmas lights on trees in June, so that is a reasonable question. I explain.

She sniffs. "I suppose I'd better help. You two have no sense of style anyway."

"Three," Lauren corrects her. "Don't forget about Alice." That just gets a mega eye roll from Cat but she starts draping soft fabrics as if she was on a fashion shoot.

Inside, I choose all the prettiest plates we have and whip up a selection of fabulous little canapés. All teeny mouthfuls, packed with flavor. It's all improvised so the range is limited, but as I look at my work, I feel a sense of satisfaction that's been missing for a while. I am making great food for my family again. All my family. And that feels good.

By now Mum has arrived back. "What's all this?"

"You can eat lots today," I point out helpfully. "I mean, you have had your detox after all."

Dad shambles in, looking worried. "Whose birthday have I forgotten this time?"

"No one's," I say. "This is spontaneous fun."

Mum's face suggests she's struggling with the fun aspect. "But my best throws. Outside." She starts to gather them up. "No, this is too far. You can have the old picnic blankets instead." But she's not reckoned with Lauren, who just puts her foot down both literally and metaphorically.

"No," Lauren says, "Jess said we could get whatever we wanted and Cat and Alice and me have worked very hard. So just no."

Mum looks like she's about to start when Dad puts a hand on her shoulder. "Let's just roll with it, shall we, love?" Again, her face suggests that rolling with it is not her preferred social activity, but she just shrugs and sits herself down on the old patio furniture that has been massively improved by being draped with expensive throws. She takes a bite of one of my nibbles and for the first time her face relaxes.

"Okay, Mum? Have another one."

"Don't mind if I do. Steve, get me a white wine. Seems a waste not to. Now will someone tell me what's going on?"

I leave at that point.

Upstairs, my heart is starting to pound as I stand outside Gran's door. I knock and go in.

"Darling!" she cries. "So glad to see you. It's been rather dull up here today."

I sit down by her. "I know. It must be. I've arranged something for you."

A shadow crosses her face. "Exactly what have you been planning, Jesobel?"

"You can see for yourself. Come on." I stand by the window and motion her over.

"I'm not sure I like this," she complains. She starts to push herself up from the chair, and I can see the effort in her face, but she strikes at my hand when I try to help her. "I'm not dead yet, child. I can manage." Once on her feet, she makes the few steps across to the window.

Below, in the late spring sun, the garden twinkles. White Christmas lights are wound round every tree. Dad's found loads of old Ikea lanterns and he and Mum are giggling as they attach them to the branches so that they sway in the breeze. Cat and Lauren are dressing up in the throws and pretending to walk on the catwalk.

"And what is this?" Gran demands.

"Just a little family party. But it's not complete unless you come."

She looks as lost as a child. "I'm not sure," she mumbles. "Is it cold out?"

"We've got it all ready. It's warm, it's pretty. There's a double gin and tonic with lime and ice just waiting for you."

"I can have that up here."

"No," I say, "I stole all your gin this morning. If you want a drink, you'll have to come with me. And I've made lots of nice things."

I'm not sure if it's the gin or my cooking that does the trick, but she reluctantly makes a move for the door. It's painful to see how slowly she moves. But she does. And as she goes on, while she still has to hold on to the walls, her tread seems to get stronger.

She takes my arm as we walk through the kitchen, but then she pauses just as we are about to go into the garden. "It's okay, Gran, it's just us," I say to reassure her. She takes a deep breath and then steps outside.

"Oh," she says.

"Hiya, Mum." Dad comes to hug her, then Cat and even Mum come over. Lauren loiters behind a bush, scowling.

Gran seems dazed, her eyes bright in the red brilliance of the spring sunset. "Come and sit down," I say and wrap her up in the softest, warmest blankets I can find.

She's still not said anything.

I put her gin in her hand. "Is everything all right, Gran?"

She holds my hand with her ancient gnarled hand and squeezes. She takes a deep breath in, holds it, and then out again. "Everything is just perfect. It's tickety-boo."

And then the evening begins.

CHAPTER THIRTY

**Observation #83:
Sometimes happiness comes
very unexpectedly.**

It is perfect in every way. When it turns cold, Dad lights a fire in the fire pit. We all snuggle together in rugs and even a few tiny stars make an appearance. At one point, we all get worried as Gran starts to choke on an olive. But then we realize that the chokes were really laughter and she's had us all fooled.

"Gran," I scold her, "don't do that. It's naughty."

"I'm eighty. I can be naughty if I want. Now, where are those little puffy things? I like them."

We're all watching in fascination as Gran eats something.

"Will you stop looking? I'm not an exhibit in a zoo," she huffs.

"Alice says that she's never seen you eat before," Lauren says, only visible by her two eyes peering out from a mountain of cushions.

Gran sighs. "Alice can mind her own business."

The cushions erupt as Lauren catapults upward. "Hurray!"

"What on earth is the matter with you?" Gran asks.

Lauren capers round the garden, a blanket trailing like a cape after her. "You said Alice was real, you said Alice was real," she repeats in triumph.

"I think it's time for you to go to bed," I say, but she sticks out her bottom lip mutinously.

"Let the child stay," Gran says, "as long as someone fills up my glass."

I should be studying. I should be checking out more responses to my post. But I decide that just for one evening, I'm better off here.

Eventually, the light fades, the conversation dulls, Lauren falls asleep and Gran complains of the cold. Dad helps her back upstairs and Mum, Cat and I start to tidy up.

A while later, in my room, I check my mail and see how my post is doing. Imogen is in a happy meltdown as she tells me about global reach and the most number of hits she's ever had. Apparently, I have to start my own blog or YouTube account. She has a vision for me! I enjoy her enthusiasm and like the fact that so many people seem to have read and mostly liked what I wrote. But I think I've had enough time going viral. The clip was one false version of me; this was nearer the truth but it was still an artificial version. It was my best, most coherent and thoughtful me. But no one can be like that all the time. I just want to be Jess for a while. No drama, no diets.

Just as I'm thinking about whether to chat to Hannah, her name glows on my phone. I accept the call, and at first, all I get is a torrent of words. "Calm down, Hannah, what's going on?"

"Oh my God, Zara is having a meltdown!"

Turns out that Matt has left. Left school, left home, left Zara and gone to London to join a boy band. A BOY BAND! Mr. Cool. Mr. I-love-your-dad's-music-he's-so-authentic. Just gone.

"And why's Zara lost it? Isn't she happy that he's going on to great and glorious things?"

"No, cos he dumped her first and said he didn't want to be tied down."

I suck in my breath. "He'd better watch out. If he does become famous, then she'll sell her story to the papers as quickly as you can say *gold digger*." I think about it a bit longer. "But that's mean though."

Hannah's voice gets a bit high-pitched. "It's Zara. Don't be nice to Zara. And don't even think about being nice about Matt. I know you liked him but he's left the band without a singer. Alex has gone all moody. They've got loads of gigs lined up but now they've got no singer."

I sympathize, but really, a very different thought is in my mind. I end the call to Hannah. My fingers hover over the keyboard. This is the perfect opportunity to text Alex. I've been waiting for him to ask me out for coffee. I've been on the verge of doing it myself a thousand times. But something's held me back. I suppose I got it so wrong with Matt that I'm scared to put my heart out there just again.

In the end, I go for a text. Sorry to hear about the loser Matt. But destiny is clearly calling you. #alexforlead Jx. I reread and reread. *X* or no *x*? Too cheesy? I tweak and retweak and then I just send.

I wait.

It's getting late.

Surely, he'll respond.

He's supposed to like me.

But while my phones buzzes from time to time, Alex's name never appears.

I am an idiot when it comes to boys. He's not that into me at all. Not sure how much more rejection my ego can take. Time to sleep.

The moment I wake in the morning, I grab my phone. Still nothing from Alex. I swear not to look at my phone again, but I constantly check on the way to school and as much as I can in lessons without getting caught.

Lunchtime. Finally. Alex. You're right, Matt is a loser but not so sure I believe in destiny. Could discuss over coffee after school?

Heart pounding, I'm about to answer straight away but then I remember that he's kept me waiting for twelve hours precisely. So at the very least, I can keep him waiting for twelve minutes. But he answers. And he wants coffee. And I want coffee, too. The world suddenly goes all sparkly again.

"What are you smiling about?" Izzie slumps down next to me.

"Oh, nothing," I say.

"What kind of nothing?"

I peer around. No Hannah. I don't want to tell her as that might be weird. "I'm going for a coffee with Alex," I say.

Izzie looks cross. "Alex?"

"That's what I said."

"But you liked Matt?"

Now it's my turn to look cross. "I was an idiot. At the party, Alex tried to kiss me and now he wants to meet up."

I am clearly not speaking the same language as Izzie as now she says, "What do you mean he tried to kiss you?"

Exasperated, I start to wind her up. "Well, I don't know if you know what kissing is but when a boy and girl like each other … well, if a girl and girl like each other … hang that, two boys can do it, too …"

"Why didn't I know this before?"

I stare at her. "Why are you being weird? I'm telling you now."

"Okay." But her shrug annoys me. Why do I get the feeling that she's not telling me something? "When are you meeting him?"

"I was going to meet him after school but we've not sorted out the details yet."

Now she really is cross. "But you said that you'd help me review that topic in Chemistry. You know I can't do it and we've got a test tomorrow."

I feel my date with Alex slipping away from me. "I did say that, but do we have to do it this afternoon?"

"Jesobel Jones, have we not always promised that we would not be the kind of girls who dump friends for a boyfriend?"

I nod. It's true, we have.

"So, Alex or me?"

I sigh. "You, of course. I'll meet him later."

The sparkliness of the situation has been rather tarnished. But it's true, I did promise and I keep my word. Time to text back. Anyway, I'm sure it won't matter if it's a bit later.

But apparently, it does. Alex is rehearsing later so he can't make the time I suggest.

Oh well. Maybe tomorrow?

Maybe, I'll be in touch.

And that's it. He's gone, and I feel strangely alone.

After studying with Izzie, I still feel strange. Yes, I've been a good friend. But being morally virtuous can leave you hollow, so I eat a very large slice of cake when I get home.

"Right, you're coming running with me." Cat appears from behind the fridge door like the Ghost of Food Past. "You'll need to run for an hour to burn that off."

"What if I don't want to burn it off? What if I want to watch TV all evening?"

"Then you'll die of heart failure." She stares at me eating.

"Go away. You're putting me off my food."

"That is precisely the plan. You were doing so well. I hate to see you backsliding."

I've had enough. "You leave me to eat my carb, sugar and fat festival in peace and I'll run for thirty minutes with you."

"Forty-five."

"Thirty-seven and a half minutes. That's my last offer."

"Fine." She starts to slouch off. "But I'll throw in some conditioning to finish off."

A while later, Cat and I are pounding the streets again. One day I might learn to run in a pretty way, all swinging ponytail and pert bum. But not today. I'm still going for the red face and unsightly sweat marks. I read that being authentic is all the rage. I run in a very authentic way, or so I like to tell myself.

We run through the park, along the high street and then up past the church hall. It's where Alex's band rehearses. I think about going to say hello but then remember the sweat patches and rethink that idea very quickly. Let's be fair, if someone is turned on by your sweat patches, it's probably not the sign of a long and loving relationship. Or maybe ...

But my silly thoughts are interrupted. Two people are standing outside the hall door framed in light. One is tall and slim and he's very close to a girl next to him. She's got long, black, straight, gleaming hair.

It's Alex.

And that's Izzie.

And then they hug, haloed in the light. And they don't let go.

My legs keep running on while my mind tries to process this. So, that's why she was cross with me? She likes Alex and was trying to put me off. She pulled the friend card. She made me cancel my date. Lots of words to describe her whizz round my mind and none of them are very pleasant.

"Jess?" Cat says.

"What?" I shoot back.

"Is something the matter?"

"No." I just keep running.

"Only, you look like something's bothering you."

"I just keep realizing how stupid I am on a daily basis."

"Oh," is all Cat manages.

"Yes, oh."

She slows down a bit. "Is it the kind of nothing that might feel better by binge-watching a TV show and eating carbs?"

"It wouldn't hurt," I admit and we head for home.

But I know that whatever I watch, all I'll see for the rest of the night is Izzie in Alex's arms.

Exactly where I want to be.

CHAPTER
THIRTY-ONE

Observation #65:
From watching most films, it seems that being a girl
means that you can't save the world. You just
make the world look a bit prettier.

Cat does her best to cheer me up and it's great to see how she's almost become human. But she just doesn't get it.

"Alex is okay but you could do better," she offers as she nibbles on a stick of cucumber. She still hasn't quite got the concept of comfort eating. We're watching Netflix with cucumber, carrot sticks and pepper crudités. Oh yes, and that well-known blowout food — cress.

"I don't want to 'do better.' I like him."

"You liked Matt," she points out.

"I know! I was an idiot."

"Shame though, especially now he's going to be rich and famous. Maybe I should go after him."

Is she being deliberately annoying? I consider choking her to death with cress but decide that we don't have enough. "Knock yourself out. Anyway, he's just joined a boy band. They've not even got a single out yet."

"Yes, but have you seen their page?" She finds it on her phone and shows me. A moody shot of Matt looking gorgeously airbrushed pouts at me, flanked by a group of clones. Now I look at him and all I can see is how perfect a boy-band doll he would make.

"He's dead to me." I snap a carrot stick to make a point. "He's all yours."

She sniffs. "I'm not touching Zara Lovechild's leftovers. No, I have a number of options to pursue."

This momentarily perks me up. "Oh, have you met someone?"

Cat stares at me with disdain. "There are always options …" She doesn't say "for girls like me" but she might as well have. I ignore the slur.

"But which one makes your heart beat faster?"

She laughs. "God, you're such a romantic. I'll see. Probably the one who's most photogenic. I'll go for the one with the best cheekbones."

"Cheekbones?"

"Cheekbones."

I sigh. "Sod this, I'm getting some hummus."

"It's fatty and it makes your breath smell."

"One, I don't care. And two, I don't care." With that, I stomp off and take myself off to eat bread, butter and hummus in bed. I may die of overeating tonight, but at least I'll die happy and safe from any marauding vampires.

I don't sleep well that night and end up getting up and doing three hours of studying in the middle of the night. So, things really are that bad. What am I going to say to Izzie at school? What will she tell me? Or will we just be very British and pretend that nothing is going on at all …

I get up late and get to school later so I don't have to meet her in form time. I'm leaving school soon, so there's not much that they can do to me now. The receptionist tuts at me as I stroll through the door at 9:05 but I remain strangely unaffected by this. Suddenly the school — which has been my world for five years — seems very small, and all the adults vaguely ridiculous.

I avoid Izzie until lunchtime. I get there early, select the least evil option available and wait for the gang to slowly materialize. Izzie slumps down, moaning about science again. "Jess, can you help me with this homework?"

"Sorry," I say, "I'm busy tonight."

"Oh." She's clearly a bit taken aback. "Okay. Another time then."

"Sure." So restrained. What I really want to say is, *Why are you such a bitch? Why did you hug the boy that you knew I liked? #snake.* But I don't. I just manage, "I'm off to the library then." I know she's staring at me as I go. But I don't care.

Later on she texts me, r u ok?

Yup.

I have passive aggressive down to a T. I refuse to bring up the real subject because then it will make it real. If I just pretend it never happened, I can manage to keep going a bit. No boys, no drama from now on. I will study, make gorgeous food and occasionally vent at the world via brilliantly written and observed posts, which may or may not go viral. It's a good plan but my heart is not in it.

I turn my phone off and walk home on my own. For all my good grades, I've been a fool twice. I think I'm so clever and that I'm a good judge of character, but I just keep making one bad decision after another. I spend the rest of the night studying. At least I'm good at that.

*

There's a party at Dom's on Saturday. Hannah and Izzie want to get ready together but I say I'm busy and I'll see them there. I don't want to go. Get over yourself, Jess, I say to myself. You're a teenager, it's Saturday night and you're going to a party full of your friends. Which bit of this is not okay? But another part of me would rather be watching reruns of *MasterChef* on TV, laughing when they get their technique wrong.

I arrive on my own. Dom's family lives in one of these little but incredibly expensive terraced houses that all look the same — everything inside is white, shiny or requires sunglasses before viewing properly. Dom hugs me and then I follow him down to the super-cool basement where there's a very shiny kitchen (which I would KILL to have), a chill-out area and those fold-out doors into the garden. The one advantage of living around here is that I get to hang out in very nice houses, though these generally show me how shabby my own house is. Not that I'm jealous.

I help myself to a drink and chat to Sana and Bex, who are standing next to the stereo, at that stage when their feet are tapping but they're not full-on dancing. We put on our favorite track and start to dance properly. I've forgotten how much fun it is to dance with your friends.

We dance for ages. I can feel my thigh, leg and stomach muscles from Cat's punishing workout. But it's not a bad pain. I just feel like I've used my body for a change. But what I'm trying to say is I need a rest. I back out of the gaggle of girls who are now busting their moves and take some time out. I find myself standing next to Dom.

"Happy birthday," I say. "Good party." We look at the large group of teenagers, all drinking, chatting, laughing and dancing.

"Yeah." He nods happily. "This is good. Times like this I feel it's okay being us."

Just then my heart does a leap and then a somersault. A familiar tall figure has walked in.

Alex.

My eyes flicker over his profile and, as his eyes turn to me, I listen intently to Dom but find it hard to concentrate because I'm too aware that Alex is in the room.

I don't look at him. But I can just feel that he's there. I want to look, to see what he's up to. But then I don't want to appear interested. God, this is confusing.

"Jess, are you listening to me?" Dom says with a smile.

"Yeah, I'm just … hungry!" I say. When in doubt, mention food! I'm not actually hungry, but somehow people always expect me to talk about food, so it's an easy excuse.

I allow myself a quick glance around the room.

Alex is talking to Izzie. They're standing slightly away from everyone else. I can't see his face but I can see hers. And she's happy. Like she's standing in a spotlight.

I think I'm going to be sick. You know how I said I'm not jealous? Forget that.

I am.

Inside, I'm dying a thousand small deaths, but on the outside, I'm discussing the fact that Dom's mum forgot to buy him a cake. The C-word gets my attention.

"No cake?" I say, shocked.

"No cake," he repeats sadly. "She said she'll get me one tomorrow."

"You mean," I say, "you're having a party, and we have no cake? This is an emergency."

Dom is clearly finding all this funny.

"Well, you're the cake girl. You could do something about it."

And at that moment, I nod my head. Yes, I could feel sorry for myself. Or, I could save the party and distract myself by doing what I do best.

Jess Jones, Queen of Cakes, to the rescue.

I start rummaging through cupboards and generally making myself busy. I mean, it does start a burst of laughing and general comments like "Jess, what *are* you doing?" When I point out the terrible situation we are in — a party with no cake — people accept that, yes, something needs to be done and, yes, I am the girl for the job. It might look a bit odd, making a cake at a party, but I am among friends. Who accept my weirdness. That is why they are called friends. End of.

It keeps me busy for an hour or so. And then the decoration. All the time, people come and chat to me. It's nice. And yes, I do let my eyes drift around the room from time to time. And yes, I can't help but notice that Izzie is still with Alex, though Hannah and Dom have joined them. It doesn't make me feel any better.

I concentrate on making the cake look lovely. And by the time I've finished, it does. I mean, I've had limited time and resources, so I couldn't make it quite the way I would normally, but I've iced the words to his favorite song over the top.

The time has come. I tell Hannah to put the right track on the iPod. The lights go off, the candles are lit. We sing "Happy Birthday" and Dom looks really, really happy. Looking round the circle of faces, everyone looks really happy. I'm not saying that I did all of that, but I did something that brought a smile to quite a few faces. And that's not a bad thing. I'll tell Cat about this when we have our next argument about food.

When the moment is over, I'm not quite sure what to do next.

Eventually, I wander out into the garden.

I like being outside on a warm, early summer evening. It feels like you're on holiday. I'd quite like to be on holiday from myself for a while.

Just then, the sound of gently plucked guitar strings strums through the air. It's melancholy but beautiful. It fits my mood perfectly. I find myself sighing, sinking deeper into my seat and deeper into the music.

Then a deep voice reaches out from inside. It is rich and full of emotion. Who do I know who sings like this? I rack my brain but can't come up with an answer. I get up and drift to the open doors so that I can see who's singing.

Alex. Perched on a stool, eyes closed, he's singing as if his life depended on it. It's not a song I recognize. He must have written it. It's all about seeing someone's beautiful soul. I feel tears pricking my eyes. He's so talented, so good with words. Then he opens his eyes and he and Izzie look at each other for a moment and all I can think of is how it must feel for him to sing and look at you and know that he's singing just for you.

Now I'm about to sob. I slip back out into the garden and open the gate. I just want to go home and be alone now. The air wobbles in front of me as big tears distort my sight.

"Jess?"

I turn. Haloed by the streetlight, Alex stands there.

I stop. What is there to say?

He walks toward me, his face soft with emotion. "Hey."

"Hey." It's all I can manage.

"Is my singing really that bad?"

I shake my head. "It was good. Really, really good. Whatever it is, you've got it."

He steps closer. "So why run off in the dark? I was going to do an encore."

I wipe the rebel tears away. "I just felt … it was better if I went."

His face crinkles with confusion. "Why would you think that?"

I'm tired of secrets. "You and Izzie."

"Why are you talking in riddles?"

Okay, now I'm getting angry. "You and Izzie. I saw you together after rehearsal this week."

Something like realization dawns on him. "Rehearsal? Yeah, I hugged her once for … oh … you thought?"

"Yes, I thought …"

He takes my face between his long-fingered, guitar-playing hands.

"Jesobel. You gave me the confidence to sing. I was singing for you."
There's a pause.

"Oh." I manage. "Not Izzie?"

He shakes his head. "It's all for you. That song was for you."

I breathe out the longest sigh ever and find myself resting on his shoulder. His arms wrap round me and I feel safer than I've ever felt before. His heart beats on mine. Our fingers entwine.

"How does it go again, my song?" In the dark, he sings softly to me again until I stop him with a kiss. And then we kiss forever.

CHAPTER
THIRTY-TWO

Observation #10:
Sometimes rules are useful. Sometimes they are there
to be broken. You just need to pick and choose.
Like a pick 'n' mix. Only less calorific.

So, we're getting ready. Again. Haven't we all been here before …?

But the big change is that I'm standing as still as I can as my mum is attempting to make some last-minute alterations to my dress. Currently I feel like the world's biggest voodoo doll.

"Mum, that hurt!"

"Stop moaning. This is couture." Or at least that's what I think she says as her mouth is full of pins.

"Couture or torture?"

Mum stares up at me. "When I was a model, we knew that looking good would take time and some pain. Now, do you want this dress to fit or not?"

The answer is, of course, yes. I check myself out in the mirror. Looking good. I didn't know what I wanted to wear. For a while I didn't even want to go to the Leavers' Ball. But then Cat and Mum came to the rescue. Standing still while I'm being sewn into a dress seems a small price to pay.

Eventually, Mum seems happy with what she sees. "Right, go and show your gran and then I think you're about ready."

"Thanks, Mum." She just nods. "You did a great job."

"I enjoyed it." She seems surprised at what she's saying. "Maybe I should do this more often." It turns out that Mum can not only wear clothes very well but she can alter and make them, too. Years on the catwalk were not the waste of time that I had thought.

I swish in front of her so she can see how the dress twirls and spins. "I just love it." We hug. It's awkward so we stop.

"Go on. Show Gran."

I head for the front room, and as a mark of thanks to Mum, I try to glide gracefully for a change. That goes well until I trip over my hem and fall over in the doorway.

"Jesobel!" Mum yells as I smile. Perhaps gliding gracefully is a step too far for me at the moment. I'll stick to flats and my normal walk.

"Hey, Gran." Yes, Gran is in the front room, watching TV with Lauren and Alice. I peer nervously in her direction.

"My, you look fabulous." She takes another look. "I know I'm getting old but that looks like …"

"It's one of your dresses. I hope you don't mind."

"Mind? I'm flattered. Now come here so I can get a better look at you." She rubs the fabric between her fingers. "My twenty-first. 1959. Lord, my parents made me hold it at the Conservative Club. Wouldn't be seen dead there nowadays."

It's such a beautiful dress — cinched in the waist, full skirt and off the shoulder in apparently "dove gray." Mum had to let it out a bit and put some ribbons at the back so that it would fit me but I love it. All my curves are in the right places and it skims over all the things I'm not so in love with. I've never really liked dresses before. I've always felt that nice clothes weren't for someone like me. But this dress — it connects me to Gran and even my mum. If I were the sentimental type, I might wipe a tear from my eye, but that would smudge my mascara so that's out.

Anyway, there's a blaring of horns from outside. Lauren peeks out and looks back confused. "There's a rainbow car outside."

Mum sees us off. "It's such a shame that Alex can't go with you."

My heart aches just a bit. In my head, I had it all planned out — Alex would pick me up, we'd wear color-coordinated clothes and turn up just as Zara turned up on her own. But it's not to be. I know I shouldn't be sad about it because I do know I'll have just as good a time with my friends.

And on the subject of friends, it turns out that whole Izzie and Alex thing was just one misunderstanding after another. She was just cross with me for trying to drop our study session for a boy, not cos she liked him. I was just being an idiot. Not for the first or last time.

But tonight is not about feeling down. Tonight is all about having fun. Outside, the car horn blares again. Sana's dad is here in his massive Range Rover, all decorated with rainbow ribbons the way we wanted — not just girly pink for us. Izzie, Hannah, Sana and Bex are hanging out the windows, trailing balloons, yelling, "Jeessssssss." Time for a quick selfie with Gran and then I'm off with my friends. Music blaring, we're driven up the hill to school for our final party. Our last night as proper Year Elevens of St. Ethelreda's School. Once we, too, were little Year Sevens with backpacks bigger than we were. And yet here we are, older but not necessarily wiser.

And school is the same, and yet all so different at the same time. The cars line up — yep, someone got a limo, there's a few Rolls Royces, about three Jeeps. Rumor has it that Catamaran Caroline is going to arrive in a helicopter but who knows? We get out, wave goodbye to Sana's dad and make our way into the gym.

It's been transformed. Instead of a dull, sweaty hall, where generations of students have been tortured, it's full of lights, music and balloons, and every possible surface is swagged and festooned with material, like it's been dressed for a wedding reception by a rather overenthusiastic bride.

And we're transformed, too. Freed from our blazers, regimented skirts, blouses and jumpers, we're a glorious rainbow of colors. While most of us have gone down the conventional dress route, one or two girls have turned up in full goth outfit. Which is cool. I mean, if you can't please yourself tonight, then when can you?

One thing that hasn't changed is the teachers. Mr. Ambrose and Mrs. Brown stand like birds of prey, raking us with their eyes. But tonight is not their night. I look at Mrs. Brown's hard, bitter face. I think back to what she said to me a few weeks ago and how I thought I'd burst from the injustice of it all.

Now … now … I'm just not that bothered what she thinks of me. I'm off to a new college and a new set of teachers. And what sort of life does she have if her only pleasure is tormenting girls? But tonight is not a night to think about teachers. Tonight is all about FUN with my friends.

We drift outside.

"It's beautiful." Hannah sighs. And it is. Underneath a resplendent summer sky, the green lawn is dotted with tents and gazebos, all linked with fairy lights and bunting in jewel-bright colors, fluttering in the wind. Groups of giddy girls and boys flit around, watching a magician here, trying different foods there, posing for a photo from time to time. Everyone is smiling.

"Come on." Izzie pulls me by the hand. "They're about to start." And I don't know what she's going on about until we reach the massive beanbags outside, all in front of a band who are about to play. It's like being at a mini-festival. (Though I don't think big hair, fake tans and posh frocks are generally the thing at festivals.)

But there's someone I can't help noticing. Zara. She's the color of mahogany, with nails like talons and eyelashes so long they keep getting stuck to her cheeks. She's all alone. This was supposed to be her big night, the big entrance with Matt on her arm so she could look down on us lesser mortals who hadn't managed to get a hot date. And now, for all her glamour, she's just the same as us. But really, she's worse off. Cos we're happy and she's clearly not. She rakes around, looking for somebody worth talking to. Her eyes pass over us and move on.

"The band is starting, let's make a move," Sana says. She gives my arm a quick squeeze but I just smile back.

In the main hall, they've turned off the house lights so it's pitch black inside. The air is full of chat, giggles and a sense of growing anticipation.

The stage lights blaze on. I've not felt like this since waiting to watch Dad play. Then the sound hits us, that glorious jangled mess of guitar and drums.

In the spotlight is the lead singer, with his hair glowing red in the white light and his long fingers teasing the most glorious sounds out of his beloved guitar.

Alex. Looking at me. Singing for me.

He might not be able to take me to the ball but at least I can say, "I'm with the band." They play; it's huge, loud music you can dance to, shout and sing to, lose yourself to. I'm dancing with my friends but making eye contact with a boy who really gets me.

"Now a slow one for all you lovers out there." Catcalls ring out and girls and boys begin to pair off. I've no one to dance with and I look at Alex sadly.

They start to play the intro and Alex says, "I wrote this song for someone special. I hope she knows how cool she is." And he's smiling at me. Then he starts to sing. My song. Our song. I tingle with embarrassment but also happiness. He's just publicly said I'm okay. Izzie hugs me while Hannah just rolls her eyes, but I think it's funny. The song is tender and lyrical and just the BEST THING EVER.

After a great set, the guys call it quits. We whoop, yell and shout for more songs. They'll be back later, but now it's time to dance.

A tap on the shoulder. It's Alex and I pull him into me. "Thank you," I whisper into his hair.

Perhaps we kiss. Perhaps we're told to get a room. Perhaps Hannah yells, "This is too weird." But I don't care. Then we dance to cheesy pop until our feet are sore.

I notice Tilly and Tiff, Lara and Tara all around, all mingling with other people, all having fun. I smile. I'm glad, cos that's what I'm having. I mean, I'm with my friends — what more could a girl want? I break away from Alex, who's reluctant to let me go. "Give me a moment."

I can't help but look at Zara.

I take a deep breath and walk up to her.

"Come and dance, Zara," I find myself saying. She looks amazed.

"Why? So you can push me over?"

"Don't start, Zara. Look, it's our last Year Eleven night. Come and enjoy yourself."

Zara doesn't know what to say. She just pouts and says nothing. I shrug and leave her. I tried.

But later, I see she's dancing. And that's good. Cos now's the time for the year photo.

"Get in! Everyone together." Everyone on the dance floor crowds together and smiles for the camera.

And I think I'm smiling the most. Cos I know that when I see the photo, I'm going to see a girl smiling at me. And I think she looks just right.

And I'm her and she's me.

And that's just tickety-boo.

ACKNOWLEDGMENTS

I used to think that writing was a solitary activity and didn't require the input of others. How very wrong I was!

I am indebted to all whom I've met at the Manchester Writing School at Manchester Metropolitan University: firstly, to Sherry Ashworth for offering me a place and setting the writing exercise that gave birth to Jesobel; and secondly, to my cohort, Chrissy Dentan, Jason Hill, Kim Hutson, Matt Killeen, Luci Nettleton, Alison Padley-Woods, Katy Simmonds and Paula Warrington — the most talented and supportive of writers. The North West Scooby Group were also hugely helpful when I was redrafting the middle section and they are just generally the best critique group around.

Next, I have to thank my husband, Dave, for bringing wine to the study and helping me in my many hours of technical need. My children did occasionally get in the way of writing. My younger daughter once said, "I want to help you to be a better writer." I replied, "Half an hour of peace would help." She snorted and said, "Well, that's never going to happen." Thank you also to my mother, Anne, and sister, Sarah, who have always been the most faithful of cheerleaders.

This novel would never have seen the light of day without the support of my agent, Anne Clark. She saw the potential in Jesobel and helped me find the heart of the story. Without her and Margot Edwards championing me, I would never have been published.

Similarly, huge thanks are due to Kate Egan, Lisa Lyons and all at KCP — the Loft imprint in particular — with a special mention to Emma Dolan for her cover. Kate, like Anne, saw some something in Jesobel she liked. It took a while to find the current story arc, but I learned so much about craft from her: she is the queen of the editing process!

Finally, my thanks go to all the students I've taught over the years, in particular 11–5 (my 29 extra 'daughters' — we never did quite get that family ticket to Alton Towers). I would never have been able to write this without you.

Anna Mainwaring

DISCOVER KCP LOFT

kcploft.com

41,8